SIZZLIN' SUMMER SURPRISE

Alton J. Myers
6/15/09

SIZZLIN' SUMMER SURPRISE

ALTON J. MYERS

To order additional copies of this book, contact:
Xlibris Corporation
1-888-795-4274
www.Xlibris.com
Orders@Xlibris.com
28542

FOREWORD

The decade of the 1960s was the race to space. Our nation had set a goal of making it to the moon before the '60s were over, led by the proclamation made by President John F. Kennedy early in his term of office. Could we get there before some other country achieves that goal? We were going to try, and the effort became an even greater wish with the tragic passing of JFK.

Our country needed to strengthen the science program in our schools to reach the miraculous goal of stepping on to our closest space neighbor, the moon. The teacher in this story became part of that national rush into space by helping in academic preparation by learning more himself. "Help those students be better in science" was the call across the nation. This was how our story began, with the teacher in our account landing in the physics program in Detroit.

The '60s had many things happening besides the space race, and this multifaceted decade dealt its mark on our unbeknowing teacher who thought he was in Detroit basically just to learn physics.

This was the decade of riots, turmoil, and disturbance as people yearned for a better life that was not coming quickly enough to relieve their misery. Our teacher got caught up in a major riot beyond what anyone could have imagined would happen in our nation.

THIS BOOK DOES NOT TRY TO ANSWER THE *why* of a riot or assess the values that were achieved in those three days or even place blame. The author's goal is to give an eyewitness account of what was taking place in the view of a teacher, who had his own interests and beliefs at stake. Hopefully, this will give a flavor of the events for those who did not live those days.

The author hopes this actual view of a real teacher will play a part in the education of a high schooler or an older adult who is seeking more information about our nation's history. This book, though it is historical fiction, does contain much truth. The chronological order is not quite as all took place. It is arranged to suit the story that is being told. The author believes this easy-to-read narrative will be helpful to anyone who seeks to understand the ins and outs of the decade of the '60s.

CHAPTER 1

"Hurray! I've been accepted for a summer of study by the National Science Foundation," a joy-filled David exclaimed to his friend Robert. "I didn't think it would ever happen; you know how hard it is for a science teacher to receive one of these scholarships these days."

"Yes, I know," replied Robert. "It's one chance in a thousand."

The time was 1967, and there's quite a drive to upgrade curricular offerings in high schools all across the land. Educators insisted we must have better students in science and math so our country could gain the leading edge in technology. The government was doing its best to assist, so they're offering help by granting teacher scholarships for summer- or year-long programs of study.

Dave was especially happy, for he had tried summer after summer to receive one; and finally, he was accepted to study atomic and nuclear physics for a six-week stint at the University of Detroit. Bob congratulated him, "You know you deserve one of those grants, for a number of your students have placed very well on scholarship tests. It can only help our program here in the high school."

"Thank you. I'll do my best. Do you know anything about that area of Detroit?"

"Well, yes, there are several Bavarian villages up there. Dave, you'd better watch out, or you'll never come back single once you've been there."

Wow! Me, finding romance in Detroit along with all that science! That would take the cake. Now I must come back to reality and prepare for the rest of the high school year here, final exams to get ready, and then grades, yes, and that daylong time of filling out reports and registers.

For the remaining weeks, Dave could only think what the summer would be like. *Me, a country boy, living in the city, that big motor city, away from the corn and soybeans. This is sure going to be different; and it's all paid for by the National Science Foundation, even the meals, room, and books. Wow! Am I fortunate!*

Bob and Dave worked through the remainder of the school year, talking daily about their future plans as teachers and how the students had done that year. Now it was off for a couple weeks' rest; each bade a summer farewell until they would see each other again when the fall school term began.

Finally, the middle of June arrived. Dave said to his family, "Everything is ready; I will leave tomorrow for Detroit."

Since Dave was still living at home, his mother asked him, "Are you sure you haven't forgotten something that you'll need?"

"I'm sure. I've looked through everything twice. I plan to come back every other weekend anyway for a visit here. I need to see the crops grow too, as well as to study science."

Morning sunbeams broke through the eastern sky, signaling the time had arrived. The car was packed. *I hope my '62 Plymouth can handle the city,* Dave thought, wondering what the freeway would be like.

After he waved goodbye, it's down the road and soon to Toledo, Ohio. Some of Route 280 had been completed, that interstate-highway program that was started by President Eisenhower a few years before; but it was necessary to travel some of Front Street, on the east side of Toledo, before Dave reached it, and the bridge across the Maumee River. It would be a hundred-and-twenty-mile trip altogether to McNichols Road, known as Six-mile Road in North Detroit, and to the site of the University of Detroit.

Soon, it's freeway time. Dave's Plymouth appeared to be doing fine. It seemed eager for that faster, constant speed of sixty-five as the engine purred like a kitten. Dave noticed a power under the hood he hadn't witnessed before in all his country driving. Up I-75, then the Southfield Expressway— my, the traffic's getting thick; and they're all going so fast as if they knew where they wanted to be, and there's no point in waiting to get there. What a change for a country boy who's used to waiting back of slowpokes on country roads.

A turn onto McNichols, a few more miles, and there it was, a sign: the University of Detroit, the Home of the Titans.

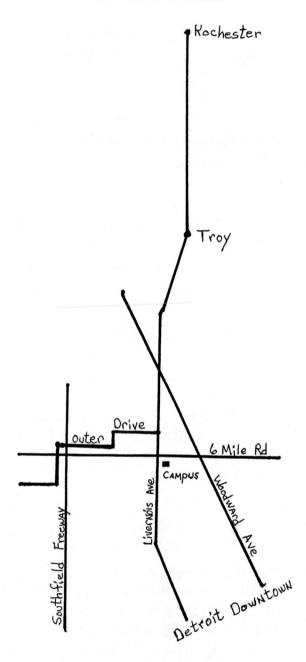

Map of Detroit Area

Yes, this is it, my home for the next six weeks, thought Dave as he parked his car in a nearby lot. *Must be a friendly place; at least, it's a Jesuit-founded school of the Catholic faith.*

After meeting a student guide and getting situated with room key and instruction, he's on his own. Dave's ready for this new life that would bear more mystery than he could ever expect would happen. Who would know the events that were about to unfold in the weeks ahead? Dave expected the normal course of study in a challenging but interesting field he knew little about, but God has a way of providing knowledge beyond our fondest expectations when we open our minds and lives to what he has to offer.

Before we go further, let's take a brief look into the future—the immediate future, that is—for Dave and a lady he is about to meet. Both Dave and the lady have similar faith perspectives, though they are unaware of those qualities in each until after they meet.

Dave was an elder in his church at an early age. Already a young teacher, his background included having served on the Religious Life Committee as a student in college and is presently serving on a presbytery committee and as a counselor at a number of summer church camps. Somehow, the superintendent of the school where Dave taught had caught wind of his spiritual interest and continued to call upon him to give the invocation at the athletic banquets every spring. The superintendent commented, "We don't need to call in a pastor from the outside; let Dave give the prayer."

The lady whom Dave is about to meet is no less endowed with spiritual gifts. Perhaps the makings for love at first sight? Who knows when Cupid will strike? Now back to our story.

After some registration in the administration building, it's time to unload his carload of goods into a two-person dorm room.

Administration Building

He's the first one there to claim his spot in the room; then it's up to the lobby of Reno Hall where a party was going on. As evening arrived, there's dancing before the first day of school tomorrow. *So this is what Bavarians do up here.* Yes, and Dave's eye caught a beautiful lady dancing with her boyfriend. *Wow, she's good-looking.* Dave pictured to himself as he looked on from the sidelines.

I think I'll like this school, he whispered silently to himself. Dave, about ready to turn in for the night, started out the door to the hallway when the young lady he was eyeing came over.

"Hi, I'm Mandy, really short for Amanda. I saw you sitting there, watching us as we danced. Good music, wasn't it?"

"Sure was. I'm Dave from Ohio. This is my first day in Detroit. I do feel a little lonely up here by myself. I think I'll have a roommate in the dorm, but he hasn't checked in yet. Thanks for talking to me. I don't want to keep you from your boyfriend."

"Oh, that's Jude; he's a Dominican brother. We are good friends. I'm from the Order of Saint Agnes. We've been students here for about two years. This is our last year in Detroit before we go back to our communities and receive new assignments."

"Oh, it's good to meet you dedicated people of faith," replied Dave in a half-choked tone.

"Jude and I are from Texas. Our communities don't wear habits or robes much anymore, except on special religious occasions. We prefer casual wear; we're sort of liberated, I guess. Hope I didn't confuse you."

"Oh no!" blurted out David, his heart half broken by the turn of events. "Have you seen *The Sound of Music*? You remind me of Maria."

"Thanks, Dave. Yes, it's a great movie, really typical of us Bavarians; but I'm hardly at the caliber of Maria."

"Maybe I'll see you around campus, Mandy."

"I hope so, Dave; it will be good to talk to you again."

A little more relaxed, Dave continued down the hallway to the stairs; his room was on the bottom floor. The thought ran through Dave's mind about romance in Detroit—how things would be. *I hope my luck turns out better with the next set of Bavarians I meet, or Bob will find me coming back just as single as I left.*

He turned the key in the door of his room, plopped down on the bed. "Hi, I'm Fred from Brooklyn; we'll be roommates for the next six weeks."

"Hi, Fred, glad you made it here okay. Hope you don't mind that I chose this side of the room."

"No, not at all."

"I'm glad to meet you, Fred. I was really getting depressed here alone in this basement dorm room, not much light coming in from the windows."

Dave's Basement Dorm Window

"No, we're sort of submerged," replied Fred. "I'm a graduate of Kingley Institute in Brooklyn. I'll be going back to New York City each weekend to be with my family and to attend our Christian worship community."

"You mean you're going to drive that six-hundred-mile trip every weekend? Gee, that's real dedication. How can you do it and still do your work here in class?"

"Well, first, I cut across Canada from Windsor to Niagara Falls using the King's Highway—that saves a lot of time and mileage. Secondly, I drive a Saab, that Swedish-made car that has only one moving part in its engine within the cylinder—that saves on cost."

"You must be a whiz, Fred, to do all that in a six-week summer study!"

Dave was soon to find out he was among quite a few "whiz kid" types with those who had been accepted for this advanced, strenuous summer of study in Detroit. What no one knew, however, what everyone was to learn before the summer was over. Only in God's good time could anyone comprehend what was to befall them in a few short weeks.

Both were ready to hit the sack when Fred asked, "Where are you from, Dave?"

"Oh, from Northwest Ohio, but I only plan to go back every other weekend. I'm a graduate of Triune College. I've been working on a master of arts degree in science and math at Boulevard State University for the past three years, and this course in physics should fit in well with my work there. You know, we teachers can only work a limited amount of study into our summer—and wintertime courses, so one has to pick and choose. Since I received a National Science Foundation grant to do it, I thought, why not? I have nothing to lose by going to Detroit. I do have to finish within six years at the university to get the MA degree there."

With that, both were asleep, waiting for the beginning of a new day tomorrow as students rather than as teachers in the classroom.

CHAPTER 2

Monday morning, after breakfast in the Reno Hall cafeteria, Dave and Fred were off to the science building to meet everyone in the classroom.

Dave commented, "My, this is a beautiful campus," as they strolled along the sidewalk. "There's the administration building where we register. I was there yesterday."

"Oh, thanks, Dave. I'll finish that this morning."

As they settled down with thirty other students, Professor Bluenan spoke, "Welcome to the University of Detroit. During these six weeks, some of you may find this extremely challenging. According to National Science Foundation regulations, we could only admit thirty students; and we are required to spread the grant through a wide range of ability among all the recipients from top to bottom. To be fair, we must provide opportunity to all teachers of science regardless of their academic background. Two or three of you were questionable admittees. That's true all across our nation with these grants, but all of you will benefit from this summer's experience in your classroom teaching next fall."

Dave shivered in his shoes. *I know who he's talking about. I'm one of those two or three at the bottom of the totem pole, but I know they won't kick me out if I make an honest effort.*

The weeks and testing of the beginning course proved Dave's insight correct. He was near the bottom of the spectrum in academic preparation for this class. He knew, however, it would be good for him; so he would roll with the bumps and bruises and take it all in.

Wow! And I get to meet the professor's son who is sitting in on our class during his summer off from graduate study in physics at Harvard. That young man is only nineteen years old and already doing graduate work in an Ivy League school. His IQ must be out of this world, but then both his father and mother have PhD's in physics. They homeschooled their son. He had a great start in the academic world to go along with his natural ability. Just wait till I tell Bob what I have found out up here during my first long-term exposure to the city away from farm life.

The days of class progressed from week to week. Dave met new friends, especially Jerry from Jersey. "I like your accent," Dave told Jerry.

"Yes, we do speak differently in New Jersey." Dave and Jerry got along pretty well together, both having similar academic preparation for this class, not too high up the ladder.

Every other weekend, when Dave remained in Detroit, they would go on sightseeing trips around the city with Jerry usually doing the driving. One weekend, it was the Fort Wayne Museum in the downtown area; another, it was off to Tiger Stadium to see the Detroit team play ball. It was a good diversion from the weeklong work in classroom and laboratory.

Each Monday morning, Fred would arrive back to the dorm room from New York City in his Saab to share breakfast time with Dave. So for the beginning weeks, things were going fairly smooth. Dave was no longer very lonely, though he still remembered the disappointment in finding out that beautiful Mandy was a Catholic sister. *Maybe somehow, our paths will meet again,* Dave thought. *God must have a reason for my meeting her.*

Working in the lab with nuclear, radioactive material was a unique experience in those days of 1967, but Dave got to do it. Even one day, while he was waiting for the atomic counter to complete its work, lightning struck right by the lab window during a thunderstorm, nearly scaring him out of his wits. But most of the time, things were pretty calm.

Dave especially enjoyed the day he got to set up the equipment to perform a Michelson-speed-of-light experiment. The professor helped as they used several hallways of the long science building to position the rapidly rotating mirrors, whose motors got going so fast that light didn't have a chance to get back in time to the first mirror. That was neat. It was something Dave could understand, though that experiment was considered pretty low among most of the highly intelligent class members who sought more atomic things. I thought the professor let Dave do it just so he wouldn't feel so out of things.

One weekend, near the middle of the six-week venture, Jerry invited Dave to go along with him to the Detroit Zoo. It was sunny and hot that July afternoon, and both appreciated that this was a drive-through zoo. You stay in the car and see the animals in that expansive setting, with ample roadways to maneuver about in the habitat regions.

"Jerry, I'm sure glad you brought me here. How did you find out about it?"

"Oh, I read in some travel brochure that Detroit had this kind of zoo."

"Gee, that's nice. Good to see giraffes and elephants looking at us as they eat their hay. It's a lot better than staying back at the dorm, reading that complicated lesson for tomorrow."

"Yes, Dave, this class is driving me nuts. For two cents, I'd go back to New Jersey and forget the rest of the course. Do you understand what they're talking about?"

"Not too much, Jerry; most of it's above my head."

Finished with the zoo tour, they headed back down Woodward Avenue toward McNichols and the dorm. It was a nice, quiet drive that Sunday afternoon, not quite the traffic that's along there on a weekday. The radio's on. A song Dave'd grown to like added a rhythm to the whole scene as Petula Clark sang one of her recent releases, "Downtown."

"Jerry, how do you like that song? It's one of my favorites."

"Yes, I think she's got a real hit coming along again," replied Jerry with an affirmative nod.

It's only a moment later that Dave took a glance toward downtown Detroit to see a puff of smoke rising in the far distance. As Jerry headed the car toward the parking lot, Dave said, "Take a look over there; see that smoke?"

"Yes, must be some store in the downtown area, really blazing up to produce smoke like that."

Both headed back to the Reno Hall lounge to finish their afternoon rest. Harry, a teacher from Maryland, of the Jewish faith, was telling his plight to others. Dave listened carefully as Jerry headed back to his room to get a magazine.

"You know," continued Harry, "it's really hard to get a teaching job in Virginia unless your family has lived there for three hundred years." Harry had been trying to land a position there in a well-known school on the Virginia side of Washington DC for a long time. He had a bachelor's degree in physics from the University of Maryland. He went on to say that the University of Maryland was one of few schools in the country that offered a doctoral degree in physics.

About that time, Jerry rushed back into lounge, with magazine in hand, to say, "I just he on the radio that the fire downtown is more than just a fire!"

"What!" exclaimed another teacher in the lounge.

"The radio says a riot broke out in a downtown bar earlier this morning, and the police are having trouble getting things under control."

"Let's go out and take a look."

That's the afternoon consensus of all the lounge people as they took a leisurely stroll across a small park area toward Livernois Avenue. Though it's now late afternoon, the air was still hot and humid as the sun moved toward its evening-hour position. Across the street was a line of stores, including Epp's Sporting Goods Store, which was soon to be the scene of a life-moving event in the short city experience of Dave.

"That smoke sure is not letting up. Can't the firemen get things under control?" remarked Harry.

That question was soon to be answered as everyone turned their heads down Livernois Avenue, toward the source of all that smoke, in the heart of Detroit. There, at least eight or ten blocks south of campus, people were milling around in the streets.

"What are those people doing, running around like that? They'll get hit by traffic!" shouted Jerry. In a few more minutes, everyone noticed that the crowd was getting closer to campus. Cars had stopped moving on Livernois, heading off in other directions. An ominous feeling came over all the students standing there on the edge of the sidewalk.

This was not good; something was wrong about all of this. You could feel it in the humid air, even if you didn't look at those apparently crazy people.

Dave felt shivers going up his back as now the crowd was close enough to make out individuals. They were moving like a wave, steadily down the street toward campus. A couple of them were on bicycles, moving just ahead of the intent-looking crowd of human revolt. Dave saw one fellow with a baseball bat in his hand; another had a bottle with a wick sticking in it. Dave shouted to the rest of his friends, "I believe it's time to get back to the dorm!"

"Yes," replied another, "let's not waste any time."

Off they went in a jog across the park area to Reno Hall.

Reno Hall

Strange turn of events in the city—no one of them had ever seen such a thing happening in America. How could it be that a peaceful Sunday afternoon suddenly became such a torrid expression of human despair?

CHAPTER 3

Harry was the first one to reach the door at Reno, with everyone following in quickly. All gathered at the window in the lobby, except Jerry, who disappeared down the hallway. What went on next was a sight to behold.

The wave hit the campus. Like a tsunami of spirit, everything that once was accepted as social norm fell apart in its wake. Society was no more, as we knew it, as teachers. No one had control of anything—no police officers, no soldiers. Everyone was on their own as the revolting mass of human tragedy approached the dorm window of Reno Hall lobby.

Suddenly, Jerry appeared in the hallway, carrying a metal pipe. He had torn it loose from one of the student chairs in a classroom. He approached the window just as a young boy neared our view, about ten or fifteen feet outside our dormitory. He had a bottle in his hand. Dave noticed a white cloth wick sticking out of the bottle.

This was not good. Though Dave was a farm boy, he'd heard of Molotov cocktails. The young boy raised the bottle high in the air as he glared directly at us through the window. All of us teachers were gathered together feeling mighty helpless. It's then that Jerry raised his metal pipe high in the air, signaling to the youngster, "Don't you dare!"

Freeze that scene for a moment! Don't forget it. It's an historic moment in Dave's life that he would never forget. Two arms raised high. One holding a pipe inside the dorm. Another, outside, holding a bottle likely filled with gasoline. This was a turning point spiritually and in the course of events that followed. This was to become a day beyond belief for anyone standing in that dorm lobby.

Thank you, Jerry. We may not be high in the academic listing of this course in atomic physics, but boy, you had some common sense. You knew enough to tear one metal leg off a student chair and use it for the well-being of everyone. Somehow, in that moment that stood still in time, a direction was changed, which could otherwise have cost us dearly.

I don't know what happened to that young boy's psyche; but for some reason, he lowered his arm and headed in another direction, bottle still in hand. Only God knows the answer. Perhaps someone in that rioting mass suddenly told him that Reno Hall was the wrong building to torch, that it was not on their list of structures to destroy. We would never know; but only in God's providence that group of teachers was to be spared, at least for then. Not a moment to be taken lightly in Dave's repertoire of spiritual experiences.

It may have been that the boy was scared by that raised pipe and with us glaring back at him through the window, but Dave gave credit to that metal weapon and Jerry's ability to find a way to use it in our defense.

However, it was the look on that ten- or eleven-year-old boy's face that set the time, the era that would never be forgotten. Dave could see it. With all the intensity of that boy's glare came also an innocence on his face, which portrayed his mission—a "holy mission" of sorts, as he saw it for his people, whether he realized it or not. All the people around him could see it if they looked in depth at that blunt projectile, hand in the air, with that powerful-yet-innocent intent to do what the rioting group felt needed to be accomplished.

If Dave were only an artist, he could paint the scene. If something could signify that time, that young lad would be the "poster boy" of an era that changed our nation's history. He represented the spirit of what was happening all through Detroit.

Poster Boy
**Illustration For Sizzlin' Summer Surprise Drawn By
Richard L. Witteborg.**

The group of teachers scattered from the lobby after that first threat of violence subsided. For the moment, there was an opportunity to plan how they would take care of themselves.

Little did they know what to plan for or for how long the trouble would last. They were living in a unique time, which, in hindsight, was a trendsetter, still visible in our cultural outlook. It was a church Dave belonged to that would be moved to write the Confession of 1967, an approved addition to the constitution of the Presbyterian faith in America. It was not entitled the Confession of 1965 or 1968 or 1970, all years with significant racial and cultural disturbance in America, but 1967; and Dave was living it.

Churches aimed at some means of reconciliation, a needed part of a believing and wholesome society. A country boy from Ohio had just seen a society completely fall apart for the first time in his life, and he didn't know how to take it. It left him with a depressing, uneasy feeling. He didn't know such a thing could happen in America, certainly not on a summer Sunday afternoon.

After wandering around in the hallway, Dave and Harry returned to the lounge. Harry said to Dave, "You do not need to stay alone in that basement dorm room tonight. Come up to my room."

"Thanks, Harry. Fred doesn't get back until early Monday morning. I'll consider it." About then, a second wave of people came down Livernois Avenue, well within view from the lobby window.

"Look, Harry. There's that guy with the baseball bat."

"What's he going to do with it?" replied Harry.

Several of the men gathered in front of Epp's Sporting Good Store. They positioned themselves in front of the big glass store window. The man with the baseball bat was handed a quilted cover, just made to fit over the major part of the bat. It had two quilted hand holders fastened so that one could grip both the cover and the bat handle at the same time.

"Unbelievable!" exclaimed Harry. "Those people know what they're doing."

I agreed. This riot had been in the planning stage for some time. You just didn't sew one of those covers together in an afternoon.

About that time, Mr. Bat man showed he's had practice at this trade. He lined himself up along that big store window like a batter at home plate, ready for the pitch. With the quilted cover firmly over the bat, he managed to grip both the cover and bat. Then he swung the combination back to his shoulder just like a baseball player does. Then with one big swing, the bat met the window squarely. *Kur-wloup!* Just that quickly, all the glass in that store window fell neatly to the bottom in thousands of pieces, not a bit of it flying out on any of the bystanders.

"You're right, Dave. They've really planned this out. My, a bat mitten made just for the occasion." During the next instant, all five or six of those rioters jumped through the opening left by the broken window to search out the store. What did they want? Guns, of course. One could already hear rifle shots every few minutes in the distance. Hard luck for these rioters, however, for the Detroit police had already been to Epp's earlier in the afternoon and had removed all the guns from the store.

Darkness was now settling in. Fear entered Dave's heart as he neared his room and realized how bad it could be for him alone in that basement dorm room with a window to the outside at ground level. He stepped back out into the hallway. Harry was still there; he hadn't gone up yet to his third-floor room. "Is your offer still good?"

"Yes, Dave, you can come up to my room for the night. You'll have to bring along a blanket or a sleeping bag and sleep under a bed 'cause I have several other people also coming to my room."

"That's fine. I doubt if we sleep much anyway."

Before they took the stairway, both decided they would like a snack from the cafeteria, but no one's there. The place was dark.

"Looks like this place has been closed down. Not normal for this time in the evening. Apparently, all the cafeteria help has left the campus. Wonder if they'll be back to get us breakfast in the morning."

"Don't know, Harry. Over there are a couple of snack machines; we can get something to take upstairs."

"Okay, Dave."

They went up to Harry's room after Dave gathered a few belongings to spend the night. Several students were waiting as Harry opened the door to let all his guests in. Dave found his spot under the bed nearest the door.

"I appreciate this, Harry," Dave said as several rifle shots were heard not far from the campus grounds. "I'll feel a lot safer up here, away from that ground-floor window."

Kur-bang!

Wow, that one was too close for comfort. Now the rifle fire is becoming a steady, resounding echo across this infected city. Will we make it through this night? Dave took a quick look through the window. A few people were milling around down there, but apparently, no buildings on campus had been set on fire.

A little more calm set in, at least for a while, as several of Harry's guests began to relax, hoping for a few winks of sleep before school tomorrow.

Harry, not quite ready to turn in for the night, turned on his TV set. He was one of the lucky ones to have that much equipment along for the summer. Everyone turned their eyes to the screen when Harry's favorite program was interrupted by a news flash.

"President Johnson will address the nation at midnight about the situation in Detroit."

"I can't believe it! LBJ talking to the nation about us in Detroit!" Dave said. "That's only an hour from now. We'd better listen to what he has to say. Maybe we're in worse trouble than any of us really knows."

If anyone was approaching sleep, that waked them up for good. One of the teachers had gone down to the cafeteria for some snack food. Upon his return to the room, they all got a report no one wanted to hear.

"They've roped the door shut at the main entrances down at the lobby! On the inside, the push bars of the twin doors were intertwined with manila rope. It was wrapped around the posts and the push door inside, so no one could open or break in from the outside."

"Wow," exclaimed Harry, "we're locked in here for the night!"

The staff of Reno Hall must have thought they could do that much for us before they vacated the building. A tense chill came over everyone as the midnight hour approached. At least that teacher shared his goodies from the snack bar as they waited for President Johnson's message. Would this night ever be over? It seemed like eternity. Who in the world would ever be ready for class tomorrow? Would there be class tomorrow?

CHAPTER 4

Midnight arrived. "We interrupt this program to bring you a special report from the president of the United States."

A moment later, President Johnson appeared on the television screen. His speech, summarized, went something like this:

"Good evening, fellow Americans. I bring you sad news about the situation we face in Detroit. Detroit is a city under siege. The situation is out of control beyond the realm of city police's capability to handle. Buildings are on fire, the riot is full-blown, spreading across the city and into the suburbs.

"I have been in contact with Governor Romney and have decided to federalize 7,000 Michigan National Guard reserves to help gain control in the city. I have also called up 4,700 paratroopers from Fort Bragg, North Carolina. They will be arriving soon at Selfridge Air Force Base and will be deployed to the state fairgrounds, north of the city on Woodward Avenue, to assist in the operations.

Additional military will be sent as conditions warrant. A detachment of heavy armor, including tanks, will arrive in Detroit on Monday. May God bless America in this tragic time. Good night."

Everyone sank back into their seats in disbelief of what had just been said by the president.

"I didn't know it was this bad," commented one teacher.

Dave looked out the window again, nothing new to be seen at this point, except the lights partially illuminating the campus grounds. The sound of continual rifle shots could be heard coming from various nearby parts of the city. Also, fire truck sirens searing the midnight air on a seemingly regular basis would prevent any sound sleeping. A few quick catnaps and Dave was up again, along with two other teachers. "I can't sleep" was the common phrase.

"Look"—pointed Dave—"look over there, near the science building! Soldiers!"

"No, those are more than soldiers. They're paratroopers. They must have already arrived from Fort Bragg."

"You're right," acknowledged Dave. "There's quite a few of them coming across the campus lawn. Look how they weave between buildings, guns in hand. Those guys are trained how to advance in difficult situations."

"It's good to see them," replied Harry, who was now up from a short sleep. "That should cool the rioters down once they meet up with those guys."

"I don't know," said one teacher. "Detroit is a pretty big area to cover. They'll need more help."

About that time, another teacher, who had had a small radio held to his ear, told what he had just heard. The report was that the routes into Detroit had been closed down. No traffic was allowed into the city. Also, I-75 had been closed down at the Ohio state line. The patrol was keeping all traffic away from Michigan. They're turning the cars and trucks back that were trying to come up from Toledo. They seemed to think the rioters may have partners in Toledo who may help them in their task of burning down buildings and looting other stores. Ohio was keeping all traffic from Michigan out of that state too. This was definitely a war zone; everyone agreed and gave thanks to Harry that he had allowed them the safety of his third-floor room for the night. Dave didn't mind sleeping under a bed; it offered added protection, even if the floor was hard.

Morning finally did arrive. Everyone was still alive. No bullet holes were found. It seemed a little calmer outdoors, not as many shots or fire trucks as last night. Rioters must have to get their sleep too somewhere.

Dave decided to go downstairs to a pay phone to let his family in Ohio know that he survived the night okay. "Hello, I'm okay up here in Detroit."

"We are too; the corn and soybeans are growing real well in this hot, humid weather."

"I mean I made it through the night okay."

"Is something wrong with you?"

"You mean you don't know what's happened in Detroit?"

"No, we haven't heard anything. Is something wrong in the city?"

Dave thought to himself, *Oh no! I've lived a whole lifetime of experience in one night, and they don't know what I've been through.* He went on to explain a little of what had taken place, but he realized no one would really know the magnitude of this event if they weren't there in the midst of it. He realized this more fully on his first trip back to Ohio, where many people either didn't know about the riot conditions or had little concern of its effect. Things were the same as forty years ago, except that perhaps there's a better stand of corn this year.

Dave no more than hung up when Fred appeared in the hallway. "Dave, I didn't think they were going to let me through the Windsor Tunnel. They asked all kinds of questions. They were going to turn me back. I finally was able to convince them I lived in Detroit for the summer. I showed them my student identification card, and they finally let me through. My, this city is a mess. There's smoke everywhere. I had to take alternate streets but still got into some bad situations with all the debris and a few people carrying guns this morning."

"I'm glad you made it back okay, Fred. Let's go to the cafeteria and see if we can find some food."

"It's still deserted. I guess the cafeteria help stayed home this morning," acknowledged Fred.

A few more teachers wandered down. One had news that the campus was completely closed down until further notice. It's a proclamation from Mayor Cavanagh, closing all schools and libraries in Detroit.

"Golly, we'll have to scrounge around and see if we can find some leftovers to eat." One opened the refrigerator and lifted out a carton of milk. "There are some boxes of breakfast food; at least we can have some cereal."

Dave's happy; that's about all he ever ate for breakfast anyway. There's orange juice too. Dave and Fred, along with some others, decided they would see if they could find an open way out of Reno Hall. "We students are all alone here," one fellow replied. "All the staff of Reno left yesterday. They will not be back until this riot settles down."

Fred found a door he could open. All were out in the fresh air. "Let's head to the science building and see how things are there." Dave took a look toward the administration building as they began that journey along the sidewalk.

"Look at that window!" Dave pointed to a bullet hole plainly visible in an office window where some poor secretary could have been seated had it been a weekday.

Fred commented, "There were real bullets flying around campus last night. We're fortunate none hit the dorm windows."

When they arrived at the science building, all was okay. There's a sign posted on the door as they expected there would be: No More Classes until Further Notice.

School Shutdown Affects 100,000

Detroit public and parochial summer schools have been closed indefinitely, shutting down classes for more than 100,000 students.

Wayne State University was closed, at least for today.

Dr. Norman Drachler, superintendent of public schools, said the decision to halt classes was made after consultation with Mayor Cavanagh and Gov. Romney.

Shortly after Drachler's order, Catholic Archdiocese Supt. Msgr. John B. Zwers said the church was canceling some 50 inner city "enrichment programs" for students.

He said personnel will be at the parochial schools where the classes are being held but they will be instructed to send home students who show up.

"We will close all public school units until further notice," Drachler said.

His order also included Board of Education offices.

WSU President William R. Keast said the university was closed "owing to emergency conditions in Detroit" and added that operations are expected to resume tomorrow. The University of Detroit also closed its doors today "until further notice.'

School Shutdown affects 100,000

The Detroit News 94th Year, No. 336
Monday, July 24, 1967
Page 8-A, columns 6 and 7 bottom of page
Reprinted with permission from The Detroit News

A number of teachers wondered what would happen with the program. Would we be given credit for the course if there was a long delay? When would it start up again? Should we try to exit the city or stick around on campus by ourselves? No one had an answer. No one had been through this kind of thing before. We're on our own.

A group of teachers, including Dave, decided since there's nothing to do and since things were less turbulent than last night, why not take a walk?

They went down Livernois Avenue but for only a block or two. There's an eerie feeling about it all as they looked on one side of the sidewalk and the other. Trash everywhere. The smell of smoke and ash left over from last night's burnings. Smoldering embers from some of the larger buildings portrayed that more and worse things may yet come, especially when night arrived again. That's enough! The group felt fear in their hearts. They decided to turn around and headed back to the campus. It's just too dangerous to go any farther uptown.

There were a few people milling around, especially homeowners or businesspeople, looking to see what's left.

"Do you see the look on their faces?" Dave went on to say. "I've never seen so much despair from anyone's face before."

The group agreed. There were no smiles around here, just anger and fear. They noticed one man with a garden hose, spraying water on the roof of his home in a valiant attempt to keep it from catching fire from the heat and embers of a burnt-out store next door.

Dave thought, *I hope he makes it—that his house will be safe. I wonder how long he can hold out.*

Border Reopens

Many Detroiters Flee to Windsor

Many Detroiters who have been "displaced" by rioting are seeking refuge in Windsor.

Police. there report numerous persons, mostly Negroes, have crossed the Detroit River in boats and are staying with friends or in motels or hotels.

Restrictions on border crossings were eased somewhat yesterday as a small measure of quiet was restored in Detroit.

Approximately 5,000 Windsor citizens, who work in Detroit and regularly use either the tunnel or the Ambassador Bridge to commute to their jobs, were being a l l o w e d again to cross the border.

Tunnel bus service, canceled Monday, was restored yesterday, but it was not back to normal for everyone.

A U.S. immigration official said it was "easier to get out of Detroit than to get in."

Canadians, curious a n d eager to cross over, were being turned back from the U.S. side of the river if they could not show good reason to enter.

Windsor police have been swamped with crank calls for the last two days. One caller indicated a boatload of armed Windsor residents was heading for Detroit. The report proved false.

Many Detroiters Flee to Windsor

> The Detroit News
> 94th Year, No. 338
> Wednesday, July 26, 1967, Page 11-A
> Reprinted with permission from The Detroit News

One had to wonder if these events, like what happened in Detroit, gave rise to the disco music song a few years later. The line in one of those '70s dance-craze tunes contained the phrase "Burn, baby, burn." What other line could so well fit the scene in Detroit, especially of what was yet to happen to these unknowing teachers. The mystery of it all was yet to unfold, which would give them education beyond that of the nuclear physics textbook.

Back at the campus, most scattered to their rooms or elsewhere. Dave looked up to the rooftop of Reno Hall. "Look!" he shouted to Fred. "Look at that guy up on the roof walking around with a gun on his shoulder!"

"Don't be alarmed. That's a military man on patrol. He's looking out for snipers."

"Oh, I didn't know we were still in that kind of danger."

"Yes, hear that shot? I know it's not that close from here, but it's still going around the city. The patrol is taking no chances."

"My, Fred, we could have got picked off on that stroll down Livernois Avenue."

"Yes, Dave, we have to be careful." Fred went into the dorm, but Dave saw a lady walking down the sidewalk. She looked familiar. "Mandy! Mandy, what are you doing out here?"

"Dave, it's you! Are you all right?"

"Yes, but this is no place for you."

"Well, our lady superior brought us back to gather some things from our residence that we didn't take on our hurried escape last night. We're staying at another motherhouse a few miles north until it's safe to return here."

"Gee, it's good to see you again, Mandy. I'm scared about my car. I have it parked in the lot at the south edge of the campus, mighty close to that furniture store that burned down last night. I wonder if I have any car left."

"Dave, I know you have," as she gave him a big hug and patted his shoulder with her hand. "Let me walk with you to your car."

"Oh, Mandy, thanks!"

They walked together to the parking lot. There it was, just like Mandy said it would be. Dave's car was there, apparently undisturbed. *Wow, God does have a purpose in my meeting Mandy.* Dave felt it in his soul. *Something good is going to come out of this experience.*

"Take care, Mandy."

"You too, Dave."

Back at the dorm and into the room, Dave tried to read some physics. Fred had his lesson finished, though they knew already that there would be no class tomorrow.

"Dave, I've talked to a Christian friend of our church community who is in trouble here in Detroit. He owns an oil company and fears his gas trucks will be set on fire. I'm going to help drive one of his trucks out of town, but I'll be back later this afternoon."

"Oh, Fred, be careful! There are snipers out there and a lot of unhappy people who want to see things burn down, including anyone who gets in their way."

"I will. I'm not going to be staying home in my room tonight, though. A branch of our church has a community near Rochester, Michigan. I'm invited up there to stay. Do you want to come along?"

"Fred, do you mean I could go up there too?"

"Yes, Dave, you would be most welcome. I'll come back to the dorm and pick you up."

"That sounds great to me, Fred."

Dave joined some of the other teachers for the day, wondering what nighttime would bring. At noon, the group raided the refrigerator again; but apparently, the supply would soon run out. The pickings were getting pretty slim. Maybe some food place would be open, but no one was sure where to go and if it would be safe.

After their short walk outside Reno, a sight to behold appeared along Livernois Avenue. All the teachers looked in awe as a tank came rolling down the street, its turret raised high.

"We were just driving our cars down that street two days ago; now a tank owns the roadway!" exclaimed Dave.

"Yes, recall what President Johnson said on TV last night. Heavy armor and tanks will arrive in Detroit on Monday."

"Oh yes, he did say that, didn't he?" replied Dave. "This is a sight I'll never forget. Wish I had a camera." Before the group could return to Reno Hall, a worker from the cafeteria joined them, carrying a sack full of food supplies.

"We haven't forgotten you people. Here's something to help you get by for at least another day until it's safe for the kitchen help to return. You'll have to prepare your own meals."

"We'll get by" was the reply. With that, the delivery person blazed a trail back to their van.

Gunfire was picking up a bit now. A fire truck, with siren piercing the air, went rapidly down the street with three riflemen perched on top, trying to protect the firemen from snipers.

Troops Ride Fire Truck

"Troops Ride Fire Truck"
The Detroit News, July 26, 1967, Page9-A photo, "bottom of page,
Reprinted with permission from The Detroit News

This was becoming a common sight and sound in Detroit. Once they set a building afire, the rioters seemingly would want their work completed and would shoot at any fireman who tried to put out the fire.

Some afternoon reading in the dorm, along with the sounds of rifle fire and fire trucks in ever-increasing frequency, made Dave wish Fred would soon be back from his mission of help. *Let's get out of here* was his thought.

CHAPTER 5

Finally, Fred appeared in the doorway, mission accomplished.

"Fred, were you able to do it?"

"Yes, Dave, but it was tense. Thank God, we drivers got all the gas trucks out of Detroit without injury. The gas-company man was very happy and thankful to God. He could have lost everything as have so many businesspeople here in this city. All of us were trembling as we drove those trucks. We sure didn't waste any time, driving as fast as we could past bands of people who looked like they wanted to attack us. Give me a little time to calm down, Dave, before we leave."

"Sure, Fred."

"You know, Dave, those trucks would never have survived another night in Detroit. My gas owner friend knew he would be on the next list of businesses the rioters wanted to attack. We were his only hope. I couldn't let him down. He's my friend."

"Fred, you are a brave person. You must have a lot of faith."

Dave couldn't realize how true that statement would be for his own safety in the night ahead. Soon he would be even more thankful he had Fred as a roommate and a friend.

The next hour was spent in relaxation and a few winks of sleep. It had been a long two days for Dave and the other teachers; nervousness and despair were beginning to creep into their being too.

This is city life? thought Dave. *I'll be happy when I get back to see soybeans growing again.* Dave got up, took a look out the window. He wondered if that paratrooper was still up there on the rooftop of Reno Hall, protecting the campus.

He and Fred finally felt it's time to head out. After gathering a few things for a night in Rochester, Michigan, they headed for Fred's Saab. One lookup to the top of Reno Hall answered Dave's question. There he was, the army patrolman, marching back and forth across the flat roof of Reno, gun on shoulder.

"Do you suppose they're doing that on all the buildings on campus?" wondered Dave.

"Yes, Dave, this is a good vantage point to see a lot of this area of Detroit. They will search out any snipers here, so we should have a safe start out of this part of the city."

Once they reached Fred's car, there was a bit of a problem. Snipers? No! It's Fred's battery. It's a little run-down. The car wouldn't start.

"Dave, will you give the car a shove?"

"Sure, Fred."

Dave jumped out and pushed the Saab down a small incline with Fred at the steering wheel. *Chug-chug-chug*—the motor began to turn over. Soon it's running fine. That one-cylinder car did not give up.

"Jump in, Dave."

They went off through the streets of Detroit, headed north, away from all these fear and sleepless nights. Dave was amazed how Fred drove. He's confident, like nothing can stop him, whether it would be rioters, traffic, or any other obstacle. This was the first time Dave had been in Fred's car. Dave clung to the seat as Fred made a turn. They're wasting no time getting out of Detroit.

The Saab went up Woodward Avenue, then the expressway, then a turn toward Troy, Michigan. Dave would never forget one traffic light Fred went through in Troy. Dave noticed the light had turned yellow, and one should proceed with caution through that downtown intersection. Would Fred make it in time because the intersection was still a block away. Though they were already traveling at a fast rate, Fred decided to go even faster, and as his Saab entered, Fred looked up to see the light turned red right above them. Zoom, on through! Dave glanced to the right; and there, parked at the intersection and waiting his turn to move, was a man glaring at them from behind his steering wheel, shaking his fist.

So this was how Fred made it through with the gas truck earlier today. He didn't wait for anything.

Even a glaring man shaking his fist didn't faze him. Fred was off for Rochester, and somehow, Dave was confident that they would make it.

Once away from the riot zone, life was different. One could feel the peacefulness in the evening air. A strange feeling of hope, which had been missing from the lives of these two for the last several days, came back. People moving on the sidewalks looked very normal and relaxed. Dave gave thanks for a little bit of good old American society as he had always known it.

The two were approaching Rochester when Fred turned the Saab on a road headed due north, a short distance west and south of the city of Rochester.

"We're about there, Dave."

"Oh, this is beautiful countryside, Fred. It reminds me of where I'm from."

"I think you'll like our community here, Dave." Fred slowed as they neared a T road ahead. At the edge of a small ditch by the road, there's a sign painted white with black letters, giving the name of their Christian community. It swung on a black metal post, much like a mailbox reaching out for postal delivery. Next to it was the sign of the T-road where Fred made a left turn to the west toward the setting sun. New Life Lane was the road. Remember that name; it would be significant for the day ahead that Dave and his comrade would experience.

The Saab moved slowly now along this road under the guiding hand of Fred. There was enough time for Dave to look around at the setting without clinging to the seat of the car. Beautiful green grass lined both sides of the lane. *Indeed, this is New Life Lane compared to where we've just been,* thought Dave.

Ahead were some homes that looked rather newly built. Farther ahead, the roadway made a loop around a big red barn, a circular drive taking one back out the direction they came, but Fred didn't go that far. He pulled into the driveway of a nearby house built along a row of homes at the right side of the roadway. Apparently, whoever planned this community was leaving the left side as a park area around that big red barn.

As soon as the Saab stopped, a man and his wife and their two children came out of the house to greet Fred and this stranger they were now welcoming into their house.

"Tom, this is Dave, my roommate at the dorm, whom I told you about on the phone this afternoon."

"Welcome, Dave, welcome to our community here. God meant for you to be here this day. We're glad you're spending the night with us."

"Thanks," Dave replied in amazement, seeing how open and accepting this couple was to someone they had never met before. "I'm happy to be here with my roommate Fred."

With that exchange, they went into the house to be seated in a spacious living room. Tom began to explain to Dave what their community was like. All the homes being built there belonged to the community. No one had anything to themselves.

Anyone who wished to build there in that beautiful setting must agree to give everything to the community, even their weekly paychecks, so all could share in common, no one higher or lower than anyone else. No one had a deed, showing themselves as owner of the house they had built!

Gee, what am I getting into? thought Dave. *I have heard of Christian communes before, but I never thought I would see one.*

The wife was getting supper as the discussion continued. "It's terrible to see the violence" was the consensus. Tom, a former Presbyterian, was an engineer in Detroit, a well-paid position. He would be missing work for the second straight day. He was highly educated, wanting to do his best at whatever task he faced. Dave sensed he was a very spiritually set person, not taking life lightly, yet with a good feeling for the beauty it held.

Why did this guy pull out of the Presbyterian Church with his family? thought Dave. *He had it all. He was an elder, a leader in a large Presbyterian Church in Detroit, and he gave it all up to be here with all kinds of—who knows what kind of— people.*

"Supper's ready!" was the call that beckoned everyone to the dining room. All gathered around the table. Tom led the prayer, the family members holding hands along with their guests, sensing God's presence for the evening and for whatever may follow. Dave enjoyed the delicious food. It had been two days since he's had a real meal, and it tasted so good. *Guess it wouldn't be bad living here, at least for the meals.*

After supper, it's a short time in the living room till the clock approached the seven o'clock hour. Everyone seemed to know what that meant, except Dave, who had a lot to learn yet that evening. It's now time to go outside as a group, sensing a spiritual happening about to take place, and to head toward that red barn in the center of the complex. They walked across the green grass in awe right up to the barn door. There's a light on high above in what Dave would call a hayloft. Inside, in the center of the barn floor, was a row or rather a circle formed by bales of straw. A few people were there, already sitting on the bales, as Tom's family and guests arrived.

Tom and his family chose their bales to sit on along with Fred. Tom motioned Dave to sit next to him. More and more people arrived until nearly all the bales were occupied. Probably in the neighborhood of twenty-five people there, all poised in silence, ready for something to start.

Tom turned to Dave to whisper a few words of explanation, realizing all of what was about to happen could bring fear in the heart of his unsuspecting Presbyterian guest.

Dave was in a state of reverence already by the atmosphere he felt surrounding this group of attentive people. He's glad Tom thought enough of him to prepare him for the next stage of events.

"Dave, there will be a point while we are reading the Psalms where we will be moved in ways likely unfamiliar to your way of worship. I know where you are coming from, having been a Presbyterian before joining this community myself. Do not be afraid. You will probably want to stay seated on your bale while we rise in a special exhortation of spirit. It will only be for several minutes during this service; then we will all be seated again, just like what you are used to."

"Thanks, Tom," Dave whispered just moments before the worship began. Dave really was grateful to Tom for understanding his faith background.

The service began very normally for Dave. Then the group began reading from the Book of Psalms until they reached a line in one psalm that had something to do with speaking from the heart to God.

All at once, right on queue, everyone, except Dave, rose silently. Hands began to reach toward the heavens until suddenly, the silence was broken by some strange utterances like a gurgling sound. It was really strange to Dave. Dave thought to himself, *What is going on with these people?* The utterances continued in undistinguishable language as faces glow through the barn light as if for the moment these people were living in another world. Some had their faces pointed upward with mouths open like they're drinking in the spirit as the random echoes continued. First one, then another, around the circle of bales, the noises varied, sometimes more intense, other times more subdued. All the time, arms were moving in weird fashion as if they're pulling down some spirit from the heavens.

I'm glad Tom told me about this ahead of time. Now all I have to do is count the minutes until this is over. Dave gave a sigh of relief as one by one, they began to sit down. *Apparently, this phase of the service is about over, and they're coming back into the world I know,* thought Dave. A few more odd sounds, and then there was silence once again. A pause to regroup emotions and presence happened before the service continued.

My, Dave whispered to himself, *this is turning out to be a sizzlin' summer of surprises for me. First, I see the city of Detroit fall apart at the seams, all in one night. Now I see a group of people lifted into another world as I sit at the edge of my bale. Gee, I never dreamt all this could happen just because I decided to take a course in physics.*

Once the service continued, Dave was introduced to the group as they welcomed him as a guest. Around the bales, each told a little bit about themselves. There's a pharmacist, a nurse, several teachers, and engineers. A few were blue-collar workers, but not many. They were mostly college-trained workers in a wide range of professions. Not all lived there, but all belonged to that community with a majority being those who had built homes of notable worth shared in community possession. They came from wide ranges of faiths, from Catholic to Protestant. Most of these groups were represented around the bales of straw that night, causing Dave to see how ecumenical this background of people was. The one thing all these people had in common was that they left those faith groups to become a new community.

How amazing that I am seeing this with my own eyes, Dave thought to himself.

He was also amazed as they went on to the mission portion of the service. Apparently, there were numbers of these communes interconnected across the country. The group here in Rochester offered prayers for another group that was having problems in Wisconsin. Fred brought concerns from his branch in Brooklyn, New York. Then there's that new group that was just forming in Oregon. All had them in their prayers for a successful beginning.

These people from Rochester suggested things they could do in providing not only financial help but also other resources, even food, in one nearby situation. This group gave not only to their own but also to others. Dave felt somewhat relieved that these people did not stay in their "other world" but came back down to serve the practical concerns of those in need.

After that phase of mission discussion and prayer, the service was over, and all headed out the barn door toward their homes or cars. *It's a clear night, so peaceful here,* Dave commented as he walked with his guest family across the green lawn. He couldn't help but wonder about how his buddies were getting along back in Detroit. Would they survive this night okay? Were things stirring up again in such upheaval as last night? Or could the military really get things under control? These were all questions that disturbed Dave's heart, though he was in the peaceful confines of this commune for tonight.

Across the road, they went that New Life Lane and into the house for the rest of the evening and the night's stay. Tom invited everyone to the living room before bedtime. He turned the TV on to see if there's any late news about Detroit. A reporter was giving an update on the riot conditions, and it was not good. Things had really picked up despite the increased military presence. Both Fred and Dave wondered if they would be able to go back to Detroit tomorrow morning.

What's happening? Well, there were even more fires being set than what occurred on Sunday night. It was true that these fires were smaller ones. It seemed like the rioters got most of the big buildings on Sunday night, the main ones of their "priority list." Though these new fires were more secondary, it's causing real problems for overtaxed firemen. They're being shot at more by snipers, so the riflemen, riding each fire truck on its run, were forced to shoot repeatedly to protect those fighting fires.

Dave wondered about that man they saw this morning, trying to protect his home with a garden hose and seeking to water down his roof and siding. Do you suppose his house was still standing, or had it given away to flames? Dave realized that's only a small incident. So many people were suffering in Detroit, with loss of life and property, their very life substance being sapped away by all these destructions.

Dave's thoughts didn't stop there. *What if his friends in the dorm run into trouble? Can they handle it again? I bet they're all up in Harry's third-floor room for a second night. Gracious Harry, thanks for him.*

About then, everyone's eyes became glued to the TV screen as live footage was being shown of tanks rolling toward a sniper's nest near the worst of the riot area. They're followed by some of those valiant paratroopers from Fort Bragg, whom Dave remembered vividly. It was just last night when he saw them weave so beautifully around the campus buildings at the university. They had confidence and grace about them that really impressed Dave.

One tank lined itself up with a house. It looked like guns were firing from every window of that two-story home. That home was apparently filled with snipers, a stronghold they didn't want to give up. It was from that house that a number of people had been picked off during the riot. Officials knew that they must get rid of that site of defiance.

Kur-bang! A puff of black smoke rolled high into the air as a tank let fire and blew the house clear off its foundation.

"That ought to shake up those rioters!" exclaimed Dave.

Paratroopers then went in to clean up the job. Maybe this signaled a turn in the riot for the better. At least there's confidence enough to turn off the TV.

"Let's hope things will soon be under control," remarked Tom as his family and Fred and Dave got ready for a comfortable, quiet night's sleep.

CHAPTER 6

The rising sun poked through the bedroom window as Fred and Dave awoke to hear Tom and his family already up, preparing breakfast.

"Oh, that was a good night's rest."

"You're right, Dave. I didn't realize how tired we were."

"Thanks, Fred, for bringing me here. I want to give Tom something to pay for my stay and food."

"They'll never accept anything, Dave. It's not their way."

Out at the breakfast table, Fred and Dave were treated to a delicious meal: eggs, muffins, cereal, orange juice. This was what they need to prepare for whatever the day may hold.

The TV news was on, and it looked like the two could head back to Detroit. True, not everything was quiet, but through the morning calm, the usual calm time of riots was the appearance of progress. The troops seemed to have a better hold on the situation, though flare-ups were likely to continue for a few days.

"Guess that cannon shot from the tank last night did some good," remarked Dave.

"Yes, we want to get back to the university in case school resumes on Wednesday," added Fred.

"You two must be careful once you're back on campus" was the theme of Tom's family's response to their guests' plans. "You are welcome to stay here longer."

There's talk about the church community, details of what they planned to do both in Rochester, Michigan, and Brooklyn, New York, in the coming months. Dave was permitted to listen in, still moved by what all he had seen with this group of faith converts. They truly represented a new way of life, completely foreign to anything he had encountered before.

After belongings were packed, Fred and Dave carried their things to the Saab, with the family standing beside them.

"Tom, I want to give you something for my stay here." Dave attempted to hand Tom several dollars from his billfold.

"No, you were meant to be here. It was God's plan that you be here with us for the night."

Dave saw the look in Tom's eyes and knew he meant it and returned the money to his pocket.

"Dave, it was all God's plan that you be here; there's no charge. God's love has covered all costs."

Gee whiz, thought Dave, *this is quite a people.* With that, both were in the Saab, waving goodbye to their host family as Fred pulled out of the lane.

The Saab drive was a time to reflect. There it was, the sign New Life Lane and the post bearing the community's name on it. Dave felt it in his bones. *I'll like to return here someday for a quiet drive around this complex, perhaps in a year or two, and see if they're still in business.* One more unusual experience to add to Dave's list of ever-growing happenings with this scholarship grant. It all started out so innocently, with an intended course in physics.

The Saab was headed down the freeway, with Detroit only minutes away. All that dreaming was put on the back burner, for Dave realized as Fred drove more cautiously and relaxed that it's back to campus and, probably, classes.

The drive into Detroit was not pleasant, for there's evidence of the riot all over the place, especially where the two needed to go to get back to campus.

"This doesn't make me happy, Fred."

"I know, Dave. I hope everyone made it through the night okay on campus."

They pulled up to the parking lot at Reno Hall, where they disembarked with their belongings. The doors were open—no longer locked to outsiders. *That's a good sign,* thought Dave.

In the lounge, they met their campus friends, who told them they missed an exciting night. "You were the fortunate ones to get out of town. True, there were no break-ins at Reno, but boy, the noise! Fire truck sirens and rifle fires even more frequently than Sunday prevented much sleeping." It was apparent that these campus people were really tired from losing two nights of sleep.

They did have some news for Fred and Dave. They're going to try to start classes tomorrow. We're supposed to watch for a sign that would be posted at the science building if we could get back to business.

Dave decided to go out and take a look at his car; after all, it had sat through another night of rioting, with him out of town. Sure enough, there it was, just like he left it. *Amazing! Mandy must still be praying for it, or some guardian angel must have taken care of things.* Dave felt very fortunate to have gotten through this much so far, untouched, except for some frayed nerves and a tired body.

He's about to go back into Reno Hall when Jude showed up in the parking lot and recognized Dave from that first night on campus.

"Hi, Jude, good to see you again! How have you managed through all of this turmoil?"

"We've been away since late Sunday night at an out-of-town location like quite a few other students. Dave, do you have a moment to talk? You can come to our residence hall for a snack."

"Sure, Jude, I'd be happy to talk." Dave and Jude walked the sidewalk to the residence. Dave had never really spoken to a Catholic brother before. He wondered what he had to say. Dave's certain Jude remembered his eyeing Mandy that first night. He hoped it's not about that.

Once inside, with snack and drink at their fingertips, Jude began his story. It's about Sunday night and a happening Jude related with fervor to Dave as though Dave were already his friend.

"Dave, during that terrible, frantic night, a couple of us brothers were involved in a rescue of some high school students from Foley Hall.

Action Line

Since National Guardsmen are actually civilians, who pays the medical bills of the guys who got hurt?—M.J.

Until the guard was federalized Tuesday, they were the state's responsibility. Now they're part of the U.S. government's active duty military personnel. As such, they're entitled to use of military medical facilities, like veterans hospitals, government insurance, disability pay, survivors' benefits in the event of death. There have been no fatalities among guardsmen, though 19 have been injured.

I'm worried sick about my daughter, who's in Detroit for a high school journalism workshop at the University of Detroit. When I tried to call, I was told the dormitory she was staying in had been evacuated. Could you please find out if she's all right?—Mrs. S., Akron, Ohio.

Deanne's fine, will call you as soon as classes are over. University moved the girls into one central dorm Monday when they were worried that fires six blocks away on Livernois might spread to Foley Hall. New dorm, Shiple Hall, is protected by double campus security, National Guard troops, teams of male students. Classes for the 120 high school journalists from all over the country began Tuesday morning. Kids are getting plenty of exposure to news reporting but aren't doing any: They're not allowed to leave campus unless they have their parents' written consent.

Action Line

Detroit Free Press
Vol. 137—No. 83,
Thursday, July 27, 1967, Page 1-A
Action Line, 1st column, near bottom of page
Reprinted by Permission of the Detroit Free Press

Foley Hall was mighty close to several large burning buildings, including that large furniture store near campus. There were several groups of high school journalism students here from all across the nation for a workshop. They got caught up in this thing like all the rest of us, and were they ever scared! We tried to calm them down, but you can imagine how teenagers would feel when they are faced with such a dilemma for the first time in their lives.

"What to do for them was the first question. None of us was safe in those beginning stages, of course, but we couldn't leave them alone in that situation with their supervisors who were just as lost for answers. Some of those kids were from your home state of Ohio. All of them were extremely intelligent, the cream of the crop of their schools, studying to be journalists; but I don't think any of them was writing the story of last night. They feared for their lives and rightly so.

Shiple Hall

"It was three of us Dominicans who decided to contact university officials to tell them the danger these students were in at Foley Hall. Finally, through the help of the university staff, we decided to move the whole group, some 120 kids, to Shiple Hall, a much better protected place and away from immediate fire danger.

"The supervisors were great. All of us helped inform the students what we were going to attempt to do. The kids gathered their belongings. With tears of fear in their eyes, they lined up at the doorways for a getaway to Shiple Hall. Fortunately, we were able to use a couple of buses to load them for transport across campus. This seemed better than walking for fear of snipers. I was in one bus, along with a supervisor. We told the kids to keep low in the bus, away from windows, close to the floor. There were no questions. They did it, even with rifle fire popping the midnight air. We wasted no time making the unload into Shiple. It took a couple of trips, but we made it without injury. It was a night I'm sure those kids will never forget. We all know that feeling.

"As the task was finished, I looked up to the top of Shiple, and there they were not one but two security guards marching back and forth across the flat rooftop, guns in arms. Thank God for the flat rooftops on the university buildings here and for the protection of troopers guarding us from that vantage point. We all felt much better after the mission was completed. We knew the youngsters would be considerably safer there, with all that extra security."

"What a story, Jude! I'm glad you told me. I suppose you had a trying time yourselves, getting back to your own residence after that rescue."

"Yes, it was a challenge, but certainly, we felt it all worthwhile in giving of ourselves in behalf of those kids. Dave, I have something else I'd like to speak to you about sometime, but I must get back to the rest of my group now. Could we meet again in a few days?"

"Sure, Jude, it's good to get to know you." Dave wondered, *What is it that Jude wants to speak to me about? You don't suppose it's about Mandy?* Arrangements were made for a gathering at Reno Hall in a couple of days.

Dave returned to Reno Hall cafeteria in time to share dinner with his friends, who each had tales to tell of what they had heard and experienced for themselves. It was good to know that some of the staff were returning now, though the riot was still going on. At least, enough had returned, so the group enjoyed a cooked meal for the first time since Sunday.

Amid all the stories, the good news was they would attempt to have class tomorrow morning. The teachers were planning to come back to resume their work on Wednesday.

"Hope this does materialize," said Fred. "We've had enough of this nonsense!"

Harry agreed. "We came here for an education, not to get shot at!"

The group was about to disband and go their own ways for the afternoon when a kitchen staff member ran into the cafeteria and shouted, "Is Fred here?"

"Yes, I'm he."

"There's a man on the phone asking for you." Fred took off for the phone located back in the cooking area. The group of teachers waited around to see what this was all about.

Fred came back. "Guys, my oil man friend Tim is in trouble! I've got to get down Livernois Avenue to help him."

Dave and Jerry said they wanted to go along.

"It's too dangerous for you to go alone. I'll drive you there, Fred," replied Jerry.

Dave pondered, *What is the trouble, do you suppose?* Then he recalled Jerry's bravery before, with that metal bar he waved in the dorm window Sunday night. *Am I brave enough to go with them down Livernois, where so much action is taking place? Yes,* he said to himself, *I'll do it.*

Fred told Jerry, "No! No car; we must walk. Would you want to leave a car parked beside a burning building?"

"Is Tim's place on fire?"

"No, but the building right next to his oil establishment is, and he fears for his life as he tries to prevent it from catching on fire, like so many smaller businesses are today."

"Dave, I'm sorry you didn't get to meet Tim around the bales last night at Rochester, but once you do, you'll understand why Tim and I are such close friends. I'm sure you understand why Tim wasn't there last night. He was sleeping at his business on Livernois, keeping a watchful eye on what was going on around there."

"Most certainly, Fred. Let's get started on our walk. You can tell us more as we trek down Livernois."

CHAPTER 7

Dave, Fred, and Jerry walked close together down Livernois, keeping a lookout in all directions for any trouble they might be getting into.

"It's about a half mile south," interjected Fred as they wasted no time in their journey. There were several people lining one side of the walk close to a store that had seen the worst of it, who gave them an unfriendly stare. They moved to one edge of the walk, trying to keep their distance from the uninviting onlookers. There's unwanted trash, discarded items some rioter didn't want to keep among his loot, that they stepped around when the silence was broken by their onlookers.

"What are you doing here? You don't belong in this neighborhood," retorted one angry man.

"We're not lingering; we just need to be at a place several blocks ahead," replied Fred.

"Okay, get out of here. We own this turf as of last night."

No one wanted to ask who owned it before these apparent looters made their claim last night. The teachers just continued in a fast pace as quickly as they could possibly exit that block.

That encounter left some chills running down each of those teachers' backs. They knew they had a mission to accomplish, so they went on. Tim's in trouble, and they wanted to help.

Ahead was the burning building, with smoke still pouring out of the smoldering remains. Our teachers saw how close it was to Tim's oil establishment as they came within about two blocks from the scene.

How they should approach was the thought that challenged the group. They knew Tim had a reason for calling Fred for help. They must be careful, for snipers could be near that area, watching and guarding their masterpiece of destruction.

Fred suggested they turn at the next block and approach from the rear. Fred was aware of the layout of the grounds since he helped with the truck escape from that location. Soon they were at the rear of the business. The heat was quite intense from the remaining embers of the store next door, but Fred knew the way through the back, and they didn't linger long outside.

"Fred," came the cry, "is that you?"

"Yes, Tim, what's the problem? Anything wrong besides the next door burn?"

"I've been hit! Don't think they were aiming at me, just at the firemen next door, who were finally forced away without gaining control of that fire. I'm hit in the arm. It happened just after I talked to you on the phone. I saw I needed help to defend the property even before the bullet hit me. I called because things were getting beyond what I felt I could handle. The building caught on fire late this morning, just before noon, when an argument broke out between the owner of that business and a mob who threatened his position on the riot.

A Flaming Wave of Violence

Flames Light the Detroit Sky During Night

A Flaming Wave of Violence

The Detroit News, July 24, 1967, Page 18-c
Column 1, upper left photo
Reprinted with permission from The Detroit News

Words were said in loud voices. I could hear even through the walls here. It was while that was going on that one of the mob threw a Molotov cocktail into his doorway, and that was it. The mob did drag him out of his store and told him to get away without any getting burnt. Guess they didn't want to take his life, just teach him a lesson. I was trying to keep my building watered down when I came in to call you. Then I came outside again and got hit."

"Let's see that arm," commented Fred.

"I wrapped a bandage around as best I could."

"Yes, Tim, you did a pretty good job. Dave, would you look into the cabinet over there? I think there's cloth in it, so we can rewrap the wound. We'll leave the bullet go till we get him to a doctor."

Jerry took a look outdoors and decided he could help by rewatering the building. It was still plenty hot around there. He turned the hose on when *kur-bang*! Someone shot pretty close, and he hit the ground. Dave and Fred saw it happen through a window and darted out to see if Jerry had been hit.

"No! You guys, I'm okay. I thought it best to hit the ground when I heard that shot. Let's get inside until the snipers leave this area. Guess the building will not catch fire; at least we can keep an eye on it for Tim from the inside until it's cooled down lower than its kindling point."

Soon the four of them pondered on what to do next. Tim needed medical attention, but could they leave the building? What if it burned or was ransacked? It's Tim's livelihood; they could not let that happen.

Dave, Fred, and Jerry began to brainstorm along with Tim. When scientists get together, ideas are born. Like the lightning bolt that hit the laboratory window earlier in our account, these men were struck by an idea. Ideas promote theories by scientists. Who knew how many theories were out there? The world was filled with them, and some were actually lined with truth. Those truth-lined theories tended to prevail, and our comparatively young budding scientists hoped they could come up with one.

Jerry exclaimed, "I've got it!" Good old Jerry— he had a way to come to the front when we needed him most. Jerry did it a few days before, in front of the window at Reno Hall, with that metal pipe in his hand. He seemed to know how to turn despair into hope. Give thanks to Jerry, his idea—*ho-hum*, theory—just might work.

"This is what I think," said Jerry. "You know the Michigan National Guard is federalized. They're helping in all ways throughout the city as quick as they can. They're transporting injured people to hospitals, and Lord only knows there are thousands of them here in Detroit. Why not give them a call and see if they can help us out here? We see that

Tim is still concerned about his property here, with
the gas tanks in the ground. If he is still on the
rioters' list to get, Tim would never be able to defend
himself, but the Michigan Guard could. The guard
could protect this area, as well as transport him to
the hospital. Maybe they would even provide a way
for us to get safely back to campus."

Fred agreed and made the call. Thank God for a
telephone book. The guard would be on their way
within a half hour. Tim was getting weak. They
could see it in his face. Yes, he'd lost some blood,
but it's the whole morning that had gotten to him.
He saw light at the end of the tunnel, and he began
to let down. The adrenaline was not flowing so fast
now, and with tiredness setting in, he fell back
toward the floor.

Fred caught him before he could crash into
anything that would hurt this already valiant fighter.
"Take it easy, Tim. Help will soon be on the way."
Jerry found a pillow to put under his head. Dave
watched for the guard convoy to arrive.

"They're here!" It didn't take long. Dave opened
the door as two guardsmen entered to assess the
situation.

Jerry said, "The first thing is to get Tim to a
hospital. He's getting weak."

"Will do," came the reply. "We already have
two others we're taking from our journey up here.
We'll have all three to the hospital within fifteen
minutes."

3-Day Riot Picture

Dead—35.
Total injuries—more than 1,000.
Fires—1,145.
Stores looted—about 1,700.
Damage—more than $200 million.
Arrests—more than 2,800.
Injured—Detroit police—49.
Injured State Police—4.
Injured national guardsmen—17.
Injured federal soldiers—none.
Injured firemen—30.
Police on duty—more than 2,000.
National guardsmen on duty—about 6,800.
U.S. Army troops — 3,300 in city; 1,400 standing by at Selfridge.

3-Day Riot Picture

"3-Day Riot Picture"
The Detroit News, July 26, 1967, Page 1-A, bottom right corner
Reprinted with permission from The Detroit News

"Good work," said Fred as all breathed a sigh of relief.

"What else?"

"Well," Dave replied to the guardsmen, "all three of us remaining here are students of the University of Detroit. Would there be some way you could get us safely back to campus?"

"Yes, more guardsmen are coming up this way soon, to be rotated with new troops from Selfridge Air Force Base. You can ride along in their convoy.

They will be going near the university campus anyway.

"You students have done good work in helping Tim. We'll be guarding this area now. You shouldn't have anything now to worry you, except your friend's recovery."

"Thank you very much," said Fred. "We know Tim is in good hands; I think he'll soon be fine."

It's only a few minutes until the homeward convoy arrived. Dave, Fred, and Jerry climbed aboard a truckload of weary guardsmen who had served downtown Detroit since Sunday. Soon they were back on campus unharmed. As soon as the truck stopped, the guardsmen wished them their best for their remaining days at the university.

"Thanks, we really appreciate it; may you each have a good rest back at Selfridge."

Back at Reno, the three returnees were treated like heroes. They had seen them disembark from the National Guard truck. "We are not heroes," remarked Fred. "We just went to help Tim and got caught up in some unexpected stuff."

Everyone traded stories of the afternoon. The Reno guys were still impressed that the three returnees, Tim's helpers, came back to the university in a National Guard truck.

Soon it's suppertime. By this time, it's a real meal, with the cafeteria staffed again. True, not everything was peaceful around here. Rifle shots and fire trucks could still be heard, but all the university people were tired of this and wanted to get back to work.

Guess they felt it's safe enough to return to campus, or was it that they were just getting acclimated to all the turmoil?

"Hope we can get rest tonight," interjected Jerry as all returned to their rooms. At least Dave gave thanks he'd not be alone in his basement dorm room. Fred would be there. No one had to sleep on floors. Everyone was back to their own quarters, trying to get into a study mood for physics tomorrow. At least they felt confident it would be a return-to-their-class schedule on Wednesday.

That night, Dave finally had time to reflect as he relaxed in bed before sleep overtook him. He tried to put everything that had happened to him over the last couple of days in perspective. It's hard to get a handle on all of it, but in his mind, he recalled high on his list his talk with Jude. What more did Jude want to talk to him about? They set Thursday for a meeting together. He couldn't help but think of Mandy. She's special. He felt it from the very first time he met her. Dave guessed, *I'll bet that's what Jude wants to talk about. I'll have to brace myself for whatever he has to say. Hope it will not be too hard to take.*

Thoughts circulated about school here and back in Ohio. *How are things with Robert back in Ohio? Do you suppose he knows what I'm going through here in Detroit? I'll have a lot to tell him when we get back to our teaching assignments in Ohio.* For a moment, it seemed like a year ago since he had been with the Ohio people. Things were so different.

There's no turning back. *Soak it in. Absorb it, and use it for the new possibilities it holds,* thought Dave. He was about to get spiritual about it all when sleep overtook him, a sleep sound enough to get him to a new day. It would be on Wednesday morning before he knew it.

CHAPTER 8

Wednesday dawned with news—class was on. It's being told around the breakfast tables as students gathered to start the day. Fred and Dave went to their room, collected their books, and began the walk toward the science building.

"Seems like a year since we've been doing this, going to class, that is," commented Dave as they strolled along in the morning sun.

"Sure does," replied Fred. "It's been hectic for all of us. I hope we can get our minds back to our studies without further interruption."

All thirty students together again, with a professor in the classroom, seemed to restore some sense of normalcy for everyone. At least this was a start in the right direction after all they had experienced in the last three days.

Dave's mind did wander in class, not unusual for him, but more so this first day back. An occasional glance out the window from his student's chair reminded him not all was at peace yet in Detroit. There went a fire truck down Six-mile Road with riflemen aboard. The siren challenged the professor's voice for a moment until the truck passed by. *Will this never end?* thought Dave.

"Now for the energy change, as the electron moves to the next level around the nucleus of the atom . . ." With those words from the professor, Dave's mind came back to the reality of class.

Despite the sound of an occasional rifle shot in the distant city, most of the day went pretty smoothly. Most people were so used to those riot sounds; no one got concerned unless it got very close. It was then the movement was to get into the shelter of a nearby building, but that happened only once or twice that day.

After lunch came the laboratory time, then the end of the school day. Now Dave's mind began to think about Thursday and his scheduled afternoon rendezvous with Jude.

I don't know if I'm looking forward to this or not, contemplated Dave. *He's a nice guy, but what does he have to say?*

Dave went to the newsstand to buy some newspapers after class. For the last three days, he'd been buying newspapers the *Detroit Free Press* and the *Detroit News. Perhaps,* he thought, *maybe someday these papers will be important—got to think about the future, you know. Each one tells something about the riot. Who knows, maybe someday, I'll write a book about this episode in my life.*

Back at the dorm, he filed that day's newspapers with the rest he had put away for good keeping. Fred saw him.

"What in the world are you going to do with all those newspapers, Dave?"

As he neatly stacked them in the corner of their room, he replied, "I don't know, Fred. I guess I'm just a nut for keeping things."

Dave didn't want to tell Fred his real plan because he was afraid Fred would think he was totally nuts and would disown him as his friend. Anyway, it was unlikely he could ever write a book; he was only into mathematics and science. All the students in that summer's physics course were totally into mathematics and science. Everyone would be happy to have the riot over and forgotten, and that was it; no future reference to it was wanted. It's back to the books and tests. We wanted to rub the slate clean of these last three days, we didn't want to hear about it anymore; there were more pressing issues at hand. Everyone was concerned how they would rank in the class after all the work was done, except perhaps Dave and Jerry, who sort of knew how they would come out: near the bottom of the heap.

A good night's sleep helped to calm everyone down so that by Thursday even Dave was feeling like a student again, reading his lesson materials diligently. Fred and Dave walked toward the science building without any background noise of the riot.

"Sure is quiet for a change."

"Yes, Dave, we're not used to it after a weeklong trial of fire sirens and gunshots. It is good to have this feeling again, but let's stay out of downtown Detroit for a while longer."

"Fred, I was hoping to go home this weekend. Maybe I'd better wait till Friday to make that decision."

"Dave, remember Friday we have a test over chapter 8, concerning laser light rays."

"Oh yes, Fred, I've been working on it. After the test, I'll think about my trip back to Ohio."

After class and lunch, it's time to meet Jude. Dave felt a nervous twinge in his stomach as the hour approached.

"Hello, Jude!"

"Hi, Dave! Is there a room where we can go to talk?"

"Sure, come this way, Jude. I know a spot."

They stopped at the snack bar along the way— some munchies while they talk should help the conversation flow—and then they were off to the room.

"You know, Dave, Mandy has been wanting me to talk to you. She has some real deep feelings for you. It all started that day we met here in Reno lounge. One look at you, and she knew you would be a friend."

"I think I know, Jude. I felt it too right away as we talked that evening. I knew there was something special about her like I had not seen in anyone else before."

"All that's good, Dave; her feelings about you are mutual."

"You mean you're not mad at me, Jude?"

"Not at all, Dave. She and I are both happy we met you. It's one of those things of life to be cherished; it can't be forced on anyone. It just has to happen. Of course, you know our time here will soon be over, and we'll go our separate ways into the next stages of living."

"Sure, Jude, I'll soon be finished with my work here as a student at the University of Detroit too."

"That's what Mandy would like to speak to you about. She realizes that time here is drawing to a close. I believe, if you're willing, that it would be well for you to talk to her the way you and I are talking here this afternoon. Could you do that for us?"

"Oh yes, Jude! You don't even have to ask. I'd be very happy to meet with her. When could that be?"

"A good time would be after Mass this Sunday evening."

"Can I come to Mass?"

"Yes, Dave, you're most welcome. I'll tell Mandy she can meet with you after the service."

Dave realized his decision about going home to Ohio this weekend was already sealed; he'd stay in Detroit. Heck with going home if he could be with Mandy. Going home could wait till the next weekend. It would probably be safer to travel then, anyway.

Back at his room, Dave found Fred in the books, like a true scientist. I knew he would do well in the test tomorrow since Fred was one of the better guys in class. Dave decided to open a book himself. Maybe now that his talk with Mandy was assured, he could get down to some real studying and at least get some of the answers right in the test on Friday morning.

After hours of work, both he and Fred decided to call it a day. They're as ready as they could be for tomorrow's class time. It's time to hit the sack after a late supper at the snack bar. It seemed like a number of the students had skipped supper that evening to study and were with Dave and Fred for the late-night reunion around the snack bar tables. Sleep overtook all of them back at their rooms without the disturbing noises of fire trucks and gunfire. That part of the simmering summer had simmered off, and for that, everyone gave thanks. Come Friday morning, give us rested minds. We'd need it to meet our professor's challenge. It's a week that had been pushed together with little time to prepare for this test, which was on the schedule from the opening of the course.

The day Friday did come peacefully. Class was almost normal, except for quite a few nervous students. The test was taken pretty much free of distraction from fire truck and other noises. Dave and other class members spent much of the rest of Friday in relaxation, some even venturing out into parts of Detroit they hadn't felt safe to go into in nearly a week. Fred took off for Brooklyn, almost like a normal weekend.

A thought hit Dave. *Gee! I have my golf clubs in the trunk of the car. There is a nice golf course just north of the campus. Why don't I try it out? The other students are getting brave and venturing out. Why don't I try it on Saturday? Maybe during that time, I can reflect and decide what I will say to Mandy on Sunday.*

Dave's bravery lasted right through Saturday. *Got to check the car out,* thought Dave. *I haven't been in it or driven it for over a week. It looks okay on the outside, but do you suppose it will run? Maybe the rioters did something to it. That car has seen just as much as any of us students and probably more, being out in full view of that burning furniture store on Sunday evening and all the other nighttime activities of the riot.*

Dave approached his Plymouth, ready for the Saturday outing at the golf course. *Don't think Jerry plays golf, or I would ask him to go along,* reflected Dave. *I know he doesn't have any clubs along in his car trunk.*

Plymouth, are you okay? Dave whispered to his car. After climbing inside his car, Dave gave thanks. It started; it ran; it's okay. Mandy must be praying for his vehicle as he felt she must be. The whole day turned out much better than anyone could have hoped. And wow! That beautiful golf course was a treat to walk across. That experience helped make the week bearable, though certainly, one felt ten years older if they had spent their whole time of these past six days in Detroit.

I wonder about Tim, thought Dave. *How is he doing? Maybe Fred will tell us on Monday.* Back at the dorm, Dave spoke to Jerry, and they decided to visit the hospital to see how Tim got along, though they supposed he had long since checked out of there.

After supper, Jerry drove them to the hospital. Surprise! They found Tim was still there. He'd go home on Sunday. It seemed he needed some minor surgery on that arm, with therapy to follow, due to the bullet damage.

"Hi, Tim, good you're making full recovery!"

"Yes, guys, thanks for being such a great help to me. I hope both of you can come up to our church in Rochester before you leave Detroit for the summer." Jerry gave a half-forced nod. It didn't appear visiting churches had much appeal to Jerry.

Dave replied, "I enjoyed my one time there, but I do have commitments this Sunday, and a week from now, I'll go back to Ohio for a long overdue visit. I'll take a rain check on that for some future time, however."

After a restful Saturday night, Dave got ready to face the events of Sunday. He's glad Tim was doing well, and his friends at the university made it through this hectic week in Detroit without injury. Now it's time to prepare himself for how he would react this time with Mandy. He's looking forward to it but at the same time realizing how precious those moments would be. *Awesome!* he thought. *I hope I can be myself and still say what I feel.*

Dave went to that stack of newspapers in the corner of the room—that sack Fred wondered what he was going to do with. A good look-through revealed an ad for a Presbyterian Church near Outer Drive in Detroit. *Looks like a big one with a lot of services. Guess I'll go to church there this morning.* Dave's thoughts were "It will be good to worship in that new setting," and then he would feel better about attending Mass this evening with his Presbyterian forms of worship already satisfied for the day.

Out to the car, after he dressed in the best clothes he had available, Dave was soon on his way to Outer Drive.

There's still riot evidence where he went, nearly all the way to the city's north side, but then it cleared up in a somewhat upper-class area, away from the hustle and bustle of the city. Soon he was at the spacious parking lot to find spot for his lowly Plymouth right next to a Cadillac. *Wonder if I'm dressed well enough to get in.* Two large gold-plated doors loomed ahead of him as he neared the entrance of the church.

CHAPTER 9

As Dave reached the church door, he found it opened rather easily. *Amazing! That gold door must be ten feet high, yet it's no task to pull it open just like the pearly gates, I guess,* thought Dave. *Wonder if this is the church Tom attended before he became part of the Christian commune at Rochester.*

Inside he found comfortable, well-cushioned pews. An attractive bulletin was handed to him with all kinds of information from *A* to *Z*. What a long list of pastors! Dave had never seen anything like this before, even in some of the city churches he had attended in Ohio. Must be seven or more pastors on the staff, with a full range of programs for young to older people, in most any category of need they might have.

I'll bet this is where Tom went; it certainly is within his range, reflected Dave. The service was inspiring to him, and they even covered many of the topics that were brought on by the week's riot.

After services and lunch back at the dorm, it's preparation time for Monday's physics class until

Dave could not take it anymore and fell back on his bed for a few winks. It's not long before Mass and his date with Mandy. He wanted to be well rested and alert when he saw her.

At supper, he kept a low profile, not really wanting to explain to the others his plans for the evening. Dave didn't need to tell anyone 'cause his roommate would not be back from New York until late Sunday night or early Monday morning. Back in his room, Dave watched the clock until it's time to leave for Mass.

He was off to church again, only this time in unfamiliar territory faithwise. The service started. He felt awe as worship proceeded with many moving sections of the hour touching him with a fervor of new spirit. As the homily was given, Dave had time to reflect, thinking through some of the events of the week and, indeed, the whole summer in Detroit.

This acceptance of scholarship work at the university had turned into a God-riveting experience that had changed Dave's life. He would never forget these times; that he was assured. The moments had settled into his being; they would not let go.

Then the service ended. It's time to look for Mandy in the crowd. Exiting the sanctuary, he saw her coming down the other side. She saw him, and then it all began again—the precious moments, that is.

"Hi, Dave, I have a place where we can meet."

"Lead the way!"

It's down a hallway right there in the church where there's a quiet, relaxing room next to a library.

"Have a seat on the couch."

Dave was thrilled that he was sitting next to Mandy.

"You know, Dave, I've been thinking about you ever since we first met that Sunday evening at Reno in June. You are a very special person to me, like no other I've known."

"Mandy, I've felt the same about you through all these weeks. I really appreciate your prayers and the faith you have shown praying for my car and, I know, for me as well; but there are more things special about you that has made it a unique experience, lifting me to new heights and possibilities. As a scientist, I would say we are on the same wavelength."

"Dave, that's what love is all about, being attuned to one another on the same wavelength of understanding and purpose. That's why I thought it would be good for us to meet and talk. Sure, I know our love is mutual. We both feel it, and I sense you understand our situation, including myself being a Catholic sister."

"Certainly, Mandy, I believe wholeheartedly it's a struggle you go through whenever you meet someone who could hold romantic interest."

"Yes, but the vows I've taken hold precedence in my life. I will honor them and still keep open to the feelings that come in personal relationships. The highest love is shown in truly caring for one another. This is the love I will continue to hold for you, Dave."

"I understand that, Mandy. I don't want you to give up your order in the Catholic realm. I'm happy to have met you and shared this friendship."

With that, Mandy's arms wrapped around Dave and his around her. Somehow, he felt a kiss land upon his cheek, and he lost no time returning one to her. In the back of his mind, Dave recalled seeing something in the Scriptures about "greeting one another with a holy kiss." *This must be one of those,* he thought.

As soon as that precious moment was finished and both were at ease again, Mandy told Dave her wish.

"Dave, I have a friend in Texas who is looking for a relationship with a good man. Her name is Carol. Would you like to write to her?"

"Yes, I'd be happy to correspond."

"I'll give you her address." Mandy proceeded to write it on a sheet of paper and handed it to Dave.

"Thanks!" replied Dave.

"Dave, I want you to know I'm still your friend. I will be praying for you all the way back to your home in Ohio when you travel there next weekend."

"I really appreciate that, Mandy." Dave then thought to himself, *I'm not losing; I've gained a true friend and perhaps a new relationship with Carol as well. I must count my blessings. I can tell Bob when I get back to teaching in Ohio that the Bavarians do hold promise. I'm not coming back empty-handed.*

After good nights and a firm handshake, each went separate ways. Dave would never forget this evening; what a sizzlin' summer of surprise this had been.

CHAPTER 10

The next week passed without any further unexpected incidents. Dave and Jerry struggled in class work but apparently learned something, for both eked out a passing grade on that major chapter 8 test on laser light.

Fred's good news was that Tim had recovered and was back to almost normal activity with his work at the oil and gas business. Detroit had settled down, but across the country, disturbances still happened, apparently many a spin-off of the Detroit event.

It's Saturday, and Dave prepared for the trip back to Ohio (with some apprehension). Would it be safe to travel through Toledo, which now had some copycat disturbances of its own?

Be brave. Mandy is with you in prayer. Dave gave thanks again for meeting her. He knew she was a true friend.

After packing the car with some additional fare and things he would not need in this last week or two in Detroit, he's off on a fairly early morning start out of the city and to the expressway, headed south. This was the first time since the riot days that he had been on his own, headed toward Ohio. How were the soybeans and the folks back home? It felt good to Dave to be headed away, and so far, there were no fearful sightings or ambushes to scare him. Soon he was approaching Toledo. That challenge still faced him before he could enter the countryside of Northwest Ohio. In the city itself, he saw one mob giving an uninviting look as he stopped at a traffic light. Dave checked to see that all his car doors were firmly locked. Good, he started up without being attacked. *Must be too early in the morning for that group to start a riot in Toledo,* Dave thought.

Finally, it's to the outskirts of the city. Dave searched inside himself. He felt it. It's Mandy's prayers wrapped around him. He knew it, and once the tension of Toledo was past, he realized it even more. Faith had seen him through, a protector like none he could have from any other source.

Arriving safely back home, Dave had a lot to tell. Some listened with intensity at what he had to say; others sort of took it in with a grain of salt. It was at church that Sunday that Dave was asked if he would be willing to give the sermon on the first Sunday after his school experience was finished for the summer in Detroit.

"Oh my, I've never tried anything like that!"

"You would do fine," came the reply from the chairman of the worship committee. "It's Layman's

Sunday, and everyone was thinking of you. We do have a packet of materials to give to you. It has a sample sermon you can use if you wish."

"Okay, I'll try it; thanks for thinking of me."

The rest of the weekend, Dave was looking over the materials that were handed to him. He read the sample sermon; it would be his first. *I will have to add to this; I must say some things about what happened in Detroit,* pondered Dave. Then he prepared his insertion between two pages of the typed manuscript he was handed.

This will do; this is what I want to say. I'll have two weeks to review it before that Sunday, concluded Dave.

The rest of the weekend was relaxing with his family. Early Monday morning, he left for Detroit. The next trip back to Ohio would be at the end of the summer term up there in the Motor City. Dave recalled during his motoring, along with what the professor said in one class, something about how the gas mileage could be greatly improved for these autos, but the oil companies were resisting that change.

Dave thought, *Certainly, Tim wouldn't resist better gas mileage for cars; at least I would like better mileage for my car.* Then his mind shifted to other things, like the end of class, the people he had met, all the happenings they had experienced in this most unusual summer.

Yes, he's happy for the soybeans that were growing nicely. Some of the farmer would always remain with Dave, but there were new things stirring within him that someday would call for an answer, and he sensed those urges would not go away.

Soon he's back on campus; then reality struck! It's back to class with only one hour to spare. This week was about to officially start. Dave paused long enough to give thanks that Mandy continued to hold him in prayer. The trip back was safe and comfortable.

Once again, this week was devoted to class. There was not much to write home about; however, Dave did prepare his first letter to Carol in Texas. What to say? He didn't know much of anything about her except that she's a friend of Mandy. He guessed that would be enough right there to make it a good chance; all would be fine. Dave even inserted a picture of himself taken at school last year.

After that was put in the mail, he realized this would be his last Sunday in Detroit. Maybe if he went to Mass again, he would see Mandy. Dave would like to exchange a farewell greeting with her. His excuse could be that letter he'd sent to Texas; he would like to tell Mandy he followed her suggestion. Second thoughts told him it would be hard to say farewell, but that's how it is. You meet a friend at school, and then, you part. *That's life,* he told himself. *I'll be brave and do it just like two weeks ago.*

Come Sunday morning, Dave headed for the church with the golden doors. Dave felt the

Presbyterian urge for worship, and he knew that location would fulfill his worship needs. The difference this Sunday had was that he parked his lowly Plymouth next to a Lincoln. Oh well, some things must be different!

Back at the dorm, he found Jerry who suggested they go out for Sunday dinner since this would be their last outing together.

"Sure, Jerry, let's do it."

Jerry replied, "I know a place uptown that, I think, is back in business again following the riot."

"Good, I'm game if you are," responded Dave. Neither Dave nor Jerry had been in downtown Detroit since the riot broke out. This was their last chance to see if it had changed. What would it look like with all those burnt-out buildings?

Jerry drove, and soon, the evidence appeared all the way down Livernois Avenue. Not much was left in a number of neighborhoods, except rubble that had not been cleaned up yet. Missing, however, were the mobs of people roaming around, so neither of these two teachers felt scared driving through.

"The place I've read about is out of the severe-riot zone. Don't think there's been too much damage in the area where we'll be eating dinner," commented Jerry as they neared the eating establishment.

Inside, they were a happy people, enjoying lunch in a pleasant atmosphere. After the meal, Jerry asked if Dave would like to visit the Fort Wayne Museum again, though they had been there earlier in the summer before the riot.

"Certainly," replied Dave, "there are areas of it we didn't cover the last time." After that visit, the two headed back to the campus. Dave had a little solitude time in his room before heading to evening Mass. *Got to think over what I'll say to Mandy if I see her tonight* was the issue stirring David at this point.

As he was off to Mass, the question of whether he'd see Mandy was soon answered. She's there, and Dave managed to find a place right back of her in the sanctuary. She signaled she saw him, but this was not a time to talk—silence and prayer only. After the service, they filed out together.

"What's up, Dave?"

"I just wanted to let you know I mailed a get-acquainted letter to Carol this weekend."

"Good, I know you'll not be disappointed. Do you have time for a cup of coffee?"

"Oh yes, Mandy!" Dave said that, even though he didn't drink coffee; he'd make an exception tonight. It would go down somehow.

As soon as coffee was in their cups there in a kitchen area of that Catholic Church, Mandy expressed a mutual joy and concern she's sure was upon Dave's and her mind.

"Dave, I'm truly glad I got to meet you. It's a joy of my life I will not forget, yet as you and I know, next week is our last here. I just want to say it will be hard to part."

"I know that, Mandy. I've been thinking this through, trying to put myself in your position: your faith commitments and how you serve in your order. Certainly, it will be hard for me to say goodbye; we both understand that. What I want to add is if in some future point your focus would change and you feel that our friendship should expand into something greater, I will remain open to that possibility, though I'm not really expecting that kind of change from you. I am a person with faith commitments too. [He went on to say about himself what was mentioned in the first chapter of this book.] My experiences in church work, of course, are different from yours, but I have a feeling for what you're going through also. I am certain you know of other sisters who have left the order to pursue family life, and in no way do I wish that upon you; only if for some unbeknown reason it would happen, I want you to know I'm your friend."

"Thanks, Dave. I'm glad we had this talk before parting. Maybe we'll see each other again before we leave Detroit."

"It could happen. Goodbye, Mandy." With a firm handshake, both left for the night. Both had felt enough emotion without taking things any further.

It's a restful night for Dave. He went to sleep believing his accomplishments for the day had been quite worthwhile.

CHAPTER 11

The last week of classes included review and getting ready for that last test. Harry came to Dave's room a day before the summer dismissal to ask if he could find a ride to the Detroit Airport when they leave campus for home.

"Sure, Harry! I'll take you," replied Dave.

Friday morning arrived. This was it—the test, then pack up, and clear out. *What a summer! We've said it before, but it bears repeating. No one will be the same, not only from class work but also from what happened in the city and to them. It has instilled a lasting and changing aspect upon everyone's life who witnessed all or part of what these days have been like. Who would have guessed at the beginning day where we would be standing in our life experience on this last day of the summer term? That's the mystery of life,* Dave realized that. He had lived moving days before, but never in this rapid-fire changing order.

How is this city going to recover? thought Dave. The destruction was horrible where the riot hit hardest; yet people had a way to recoup, realign life in hope, which appeared in mysterious and persistent ways. It may take years, but these good people will find a way to rebuild and remold their lives.

Back at his room, Dave gathered up everything from each dusty corner, blowing off any heavy dust before he packed the items in his car. Fred's already in the Saab as Dave carried out his last load, and they waved goodbye. Fred never did waste any time. He would probably be halfway to Brooklyn before Dave got Harry to the Detroit Airport.

Dave took time to eat dinner with Harry in Reno Hall cafeteria before loading Harry's suitcases in the car. This last dinner was not on the summer meal ticket, but both were happy to pay for it rather than searching out some other dining spot. Several other teachers were also in Reno, apparently having flights out of Detroit later in the afternoon.

Talk was about the summer and plans with the new teaching year soon to begin. Some were concerned the racial disturbances may affect their areas of the country too in the year ahead. They didn't want to go through what has happened here, but it was possible that that challenge may lie ahead of them.

One by one, all cleared out and said goodbye to one another, to Reno Hall, and to the Motor City. Dave and Harry climbed in the Plymouth and headed for the airport. Once there, Harry gave directions to the terminal. Harry knew from his arrival at the beginning of the summer; he never left Detroit during this whole summer course. It's Dave's first trip to the Detroit Airport. He willingly accepted Harry's direction, then shared in carrying suitcases to the lobby. The wait was not too great.

"We timed this pretty good," commented Harry.

"Yes, I'm glad you know the way. By the way, I really appreciate your putting me up in your room during those riot nights. I'm sure the others who shared your third-floor room feel the same way."

(Harry, for some reason, was about the only class member who had a room to himself. Perhaps he was the one extra class member left over, but for whatever reason, all gave thanks he shared his space.)

"Thanks, Dave. I was happy to do it." About then, "all aboard" signal came, and Harry waved goodbye with Dave there to wish him well as he departed.

Dave began to walk out of the lobby when— you would never guess who greeted him. It's Jude and Mandy!

"Hi, Dave, we didn't expect to see you here."

"Mandy and Jude, it's great to see you! I brought a classmate here so he could catch his flight to Maryland; then it's back to Ohio in my Plymouth."

"We're flying to Dallas where we'll meet community members to take us to our residences. We both start new assignments in Texas."

"I'll be praying for you," replied Dave. *After all, Mandy has been praying a lot for me,* thought Dave.

After an exchange of well-wishes, firm handshakes were given, and then with waves of goodbye, all were off to become homeward.

The return to Ohio began a new phase of summer for Dave in the few weeks before teaching duties resumed at the high school. Sure, there's some unwinding to do; however, with Sunday only a day away, it's get ready for that first sermon. True, it's mostly a manufactured one, but Dave still needed to review it, along with the part he had added.

Dave, in his best suit, went to church wondering how all this would turn out. When time came to produce a sermon for the congregation, he found his knees a little shaky, and his first words did not come out very securely. However, after the first page, all was much better. Dave felt more confident when he began his inserted addition to the sermon, for this was the part he had lived through. This was the part that had become ingrained in his being, not to be forgotten.

After church, people seemed to like what he had done. In all, it turned into an encouraging day that would shape future events in Dave's perspective for years to come.

The rest of the short weeks before school, Dave watched the soybeans and corn grow, something he longed for a number of times during those tense Detroit days.

There's some disappointment with some of the people he talked to, who did not understand what the Detroit experience had meant in Dave's life. He must be patient with them. He realized their lives had changed little while the burdens of a new vision of society were upon his shoulders. It's time to assess how he would deal with the teachers and students when the fall term began in a few weeks. They too had new experiences, quite likely very different from Dave's. He'd never be able to fully relate his to them, but he knew the school year would soon take precedence, and the summer would rapidly be shoved into the past, so he saw no great problems there.

Finally, school day arrived. "Hi, Bob!"

"You look good, Dave. Did you have a good summer?"

"Yes, Bob, Detroit has a good school up there though the riot caused some difficulties."

"I heard about it on the radio," replied Bob. "I'm glad you're back home with us here okay."

Dave figured that's far enough to go with that topic. Unless he's asked more, he'd not bring up the subject again. There was no point pressing a topic others had not experienced or could appreciate the way he did. It's his to remember, his to deal with in this rural country community. Perhaps one time he could talk about his seeing the Tigers play because a number of the teachers and students were baseball fans—that would go over pretty well. Dave did see how the owners had revamped the stadium with changes in seating and repainting this year. He was there not long after it had reopened in this 1967 season, and they changed the name from

Briggs Stadium to Tiger Stadium. A number of teachers and kids were interested in that, and the superintendent was happy that Dave now knew a little more about physics.

The school year settled into its usual routine, but not long into the year, Dave was reminded of Detroit when in the mail came a letter from Carol. He read it anxiously. She was happy he wrote to her, for Mandy was one of her best friends. Dave was happy and willing to correspond. Maybe he could keep tabs a little on Mandy by exchanging letters with Carol though he knew he must not let that get into the way of a new relationship.

During those beginning weeks of school, Dave felt inner motivation about his summer experience of seeing society fall apart in Detroit during those July days from 24 to 26. He must tell his story some way, for it burned inside him. Dave saw an offer from a company who provided guidance for anyone who wanted to write a book. *Maybe this is the way I could tell people what I know about our society in these days,* thought Dave. *I must tell people society is not as secure as they think it is. Society can fall apart right in front of them—I saw it happen with my own eyes.*

Dave sent a letter to the address in the ad. Soon he had a phone call. A representative would meet him at his house.

When the appointed evening came, a man arrived at the door. Dave invited him in, and they began to talk. One detail after another was given about writing, and Dave soaked it all in. "It would not be easy" was the theme. You had to be good at writing, and you had to become known for the topic you're writing about for a publisher to accept your work. "It is also costly, and you're taking a risk your work will not be accepted," came the news from the representative visiting in Dave's home.

The representative discouraged Dave since he had no experience in writing. In the year 1967, one had to convince a publisher to have your work appear before the public. The task looked overwhelming to Dave, and he decided to lay it aside. *I will keep the newspapers,* Dave whispered to himself. He then thanked the company representative and sent him on his way. Dave now knew what he would be up against should he ever try that venture.

CHAPTER 12

Some will say I'm out of my story as I begin chapter 12, and they are right. However, I want to toss in a thought or two related to the theme the story has sought to reveal.

The nature and trials of our human living, particularly in the times of 1967 in America, had left lasting marks upon who we are in this day. A few of our older generation, who were already born by 1967, know in firsthand account some of the incidents I speak about in this book, either by eyewitness or by reading in newspapers or hearing through media. The disturbances of the '60s actually touched some with eyewitness evidence of what went on, but the younger of us see those times mostly through the eyes of historians without having the benefit of being there in person.

It is my hope that this book has given a flavor of the times for the benefit of those who may not have known the gravity of the events. Hundreds of thousands were touched by it in Detroit, from student to older adult. Millions were affected across our nation whose stories are passed on to future generations.

I'm glad Dave asked me to write his story, the story he was unable to write due to the overwhelming odds whether it would ever be published. I am happy Dave kept the newspapers and loaned them to me; it helped greatly in writing this historical fiction novel. Again, thanks to the *Detroit News* and the *Detroit Free Press* for granting permission to reproduce articles from their newspapers for inclusion in this book.

The times were real, perhaps even surreal to use modern terms, often beyond the realm of any human expectation. We can only reflect now and try to soak in the spiritual meanings and absorb the new nuances of life that exist for us in this day because of those times of turbulence.

For the story of Dave, a schoolteacher undergoing an unusual summer of graduate study in Detroit, it is a major stepping stone to unlock many important new adventures in his future days. This story, of course, stops with the end of 1967. If for some reason, more is wished to be known, the possibility exists some future writing might occur if conditions warrant.

An interesting thought occurred to me, perhaps because of my musical interest and enjoyment. I think Dave would have been helped by a song that came out four or five years later in the early '70s, which could have expressed his feelings for Mandy more completely than he was able to tell her. The song "Betcha By Golly Wow!" had a theme that conveyed the deep expression of love that suddenly fell upon the two from the moment they met. However, Dave and Mandy met five years too soon for that particular song to guide their moments. A song like "Up, Up, and Away" did exist and perhaps helped lift their thoughts, like the red air-balloon ride portrayed in its message.

Well, enough said from my own thought book. Let's rejoin our story for the closing part of 1967. Dave was teaching well into the first semester of school when the mailman delivered a return letter from Carol.

It's good news! She's happy with his letter and picture. "Why not come to Texas?" was her response. Dave was glad she had responded and began thinking over when it would work out for a meeting. He didn't want to fly—he's scared of that. It's too far to drive comfortably, but then there's the train. Dave liked trains; that's the way he thought would be best.

A few more communications were passed, and an agreement was reached for a Christmas vacation meeting while Dave had a couple of weeks off from school. The weeks in between fly past pretty quickly with anticipation of this new event for both their lives.

After Christmas with the family, he was all aboard! It's off to San Antonio. It should be nice there after all this snow in the Northland. Dave really enjoyed looking out of the train windows at the changing scenes of the countryside. It's a good change from being in the classroom. Soon the day passed. On through Chicago, on through Kansas, on through the flatlands. Look! No trees! Then the train went south through Oklahoma.

After a couple of days, he's in San Antonio, ready to meet Carol at the train station. Would he be able to recognize her from the picture she sent? That question was soon answered as he departed from the train and milled through the waiting crowd.

"Hello, are you Dave?"

"Yes, you must be Carol."

"The pictures worked quite well. Dave, I'm glad we exchanged them. Come with me; my car is just over there in the parking lot."

The two walked to Carol's Chevy, and they went away to her apartment. The day was spent getting acquainted. She seemed nice, but not like Mandy, who was also in this city. Dave was surprised when Carol suggested they have dinner that evening with Mandy. Dave thought, *Carol must be pretty brave to suggest such a thing when she knows I'm a friend of Mandy.*

After lunch, Carol took Dave on an afternoon tour of the city. *So many nice scenes here—the River Walk, the Alamo—it's really very thoughtful of Carol to plan such an afternoon. It's a lot of entertainment, but will we get along when this excitement is over?* Dave thought.

There was little more informative talking but lacking in romantic interest, and the time arrived for the two to meet Mandy for the evening dinner. This was what Dave was looking forward to. He tried to suppress those feelings for he knew he owed the time to Carol. In fact, this whole Texas journey was because of her; yet trying as hard as he could, Dave realized deep inside himself his real interest was with Mandy. Within himself swelled a gratitude to Carol for permitting him to see Mandy again.

Carol drove the two for the rendezvous in a nice restaurant conducive to relaxed conversation. Mandy's waiting for them, and when they met, hugs went all around the three.

"Hi, Dave, I'm glad you traveled okay and have met my friend Carol."

"Oh yes, Mandy! It's so good to see you again too!" replied Dave with one happy grin beaming across his face.

Mandy turned to Carol. "We've just got to tell you some things that happened to us in Detroit last summer."

"Oh yes," said Dave. "Remember those tanks rolling down Livernois Avenue, their turrets raised high?"

"Did they shoot at you?" asked Carol.

"No," replied Mandy, "but they surely did scare us. We kept out of their way."

Dave inserted, "I saw one blew a house off its foundation, on TV, that is. It was hard to believe that kind of thing was happening in America. I will never forget seeing those paratroopers from Fort

Bragg, North Carolina, come across campus that Sunday night. Those scenes are etched into my being."

"I met a family who lost a loved one to a sniper fire in the riot," commented Mandy. "Just think there were thirty-six people killed during those three hectic days."

"A group of us on campus rescued an injured person the third day, a friend of my roommate," replied Dave.

"My, you two really did have some amazing times in Detroit," said Carol.

Carol, at this point, didn't realize what real moments of loving Dave and Mandy had last summer. Nothing was said of that, real as it was. That aspect of the summer was better left unsaid at this stage of Carol's knowing Dave.

Dave then recalled something that touched him in a deep spiritually moving fashion. A tear began to roll down his cheek as he choked, beginning to tell the most impressive sight of the whole riot in his eyes. Mandy reached over to clutch his hand as he began to talk, seeming to know her loved one was having real trouble to say what he was about to tell.

"You know," Dave began, "there was that intent young boy, probably only eleven or twelve years old, who carried a Molotov cocktail right to our dorm window. He was positioned outside only ten or fifteen feet from us, glaring intently at all of us standing there, who were looking back at him through the window, wondering what was going to happen next.

"That boy had such an innocent look on his face. He seemed to be trying to tell us without words that he had a mission to accomplish for his people. The child had to express what his people had felt through years spent being oppressed by the society around them. It was time to revolt, to call attention to their plight, and this kid was in no way going to let them down.

"Really, there was no one else standing close by him as he looked at us, his hand raised high with that wick-laden bottle. It was his decision rather to throw it through the window at us and set us on fire or leave us alone. He didn't really seem angry, just determined to do his job for his downtrodden people. It must have been us or Jerry, our determined classmate, who changed his mind, or maybe it was his young conscience within him that did it; but he did go on his way to other things, leaving us untouched, safely standing there in the dorm. It's a scene I cannot forget. For me, it signifies the whole spirit of the racial disturbance in Detroit and perhaps of the whole nation, as it is happening here in the '60s."

A great sigh of relief came over Dave as he finished his story. Both ladies sat there stunned by the feeling Dave emitted as he told his heartfelt story.

This had to be the conclusion of the Texas day as all three finished their dinner to return to their respective residences for the evening. The train would soon be arriving to return Dave to Ohio. Mandy and Carol would go to the station to see him off.

The time approached as Carol drove Dave to meet the train.

"I'm glad I got to know you, Carol. Thanks for being such a nice host."

"You're welcome, Dave. I enjoyed meeting you too. Let's write to one another and see where it goes from there."

"That sounds good, Carol. I'll do that."

As they reached the station, Dave opened the car door for Carol and offered his arm as they walked together to the terminal. Mandy met them there. Dave, Mandy, and Carol shared in a three-way hug. Dave waved to both as he boarded the train. He continued to wave to them through the window until the train was completely out of the station and away from view.

My, that was a nice vacation, Dave murmured to himself, *and Mandy is still as lovely as the day I met her.*

It took two days to get back to Ohio by way of Chicago. Didn't all trains go through Chicago? It seemed that way to Dave as he made a transfer in the crowded terminal. Then he arrived in Ohio. He was back at home to relax for a day until the New Year came in. Well, that's the end of 1967. What a year it had been for Dave and for our whole country. We'd never be the same. The people of Detroit knew that, as did anyone else who lived those days.

What would the future be? Dave and the others would step into 1968, but that's for another book to tell. This one ends with 1967.

There is some spiritual answer to all of this, some mysterious solution, that only the future will reveal; and perhaps that's in the beauty and challenge of a society, which holds together through a peaceful hope, that offers freedom to become all that our natural gifts can bring forth to share.

Dave was a better physics teacher. He also had a new grip on life that was not present before. He was sure his friends had also grown. All thirty science teachers in that summer course had found much more than they expected from the Detroit experience. It was good they were together to learn all that they learned in a sizzlin' summer surprise.